DEAD
HOT

ISBN-13: 978-1-63696-170-5
ISBN-10: 1-63696-170-3

Cover design by: Damonza
Printed in the United States of America

DAVID ARCHER
BLAKE BANNER

DEAD
HOT

AN ALEX
MASON
THRILLER

R
RIGHT HOUSE

ALEX MASON SERIES

Odin

Ice Cold Spy

Mason's Law

Assets and Liabilities

Russian Roulette

Executive Order

Dead Man Talking

All the King's Men

Flashpoint

Brotherhood of the Goat

Dead Hot

PROLOGUE

P ete Justin was an American patriot. He made the fine distinction between loving your country and loving the politicians who made it their daily business to rape and abuse that country. He was not a Liberal or a Conservative, he was not a Democrat or a Republican. He was an American who loved his country with an unquenchable passion, and hated the men and women who ran it with what he thought of as a Newtonian passion. Because it was equal and opposite to his love for his country.

He had known since he was a boy that his spiritual home was, and always would be, Wyoming. They called it the Cowboy State because of all the beef, but those who knew it well knew it was the Miners' State. It was what was under the ground that made Wyoming special; it was what created the real wealth, and held it in perpetual peril. There was gold here, there was coal here, and then there was the Caldera. Yet, where the doomsayers pointed to the green revolution as the demise of Wyoming's coal, or the long overdue eruption of the Caldera as the coming end of humanity, Pete saw Wyoming as a kind of Rivendell: a vast area of close to one hundred thousand square miles, with a population of one sixteenth that of New York – and over a quarter of those were in the three main cities of Cheyenne, Casper and Laramie. It was a small Eden virtually untouched by multiculturalism, Woke inclusiveness or rainbow acronyms. This, Pete believed, was the heart and soul of America.

These thoughts drifted through his mind unchallenged and unquestioned, accepted as truth, as he rode steadily up through the pinewoods, leaving behind him the Caldera Rim and the Gibbons River.

He had driven just over a hundred miles from Jackson, as he did every week from April to September, as he had for the last ten years. He'd left his truck at Iron Springs and collected his horse from the lodge the little known Federal Office of the Environment had given him there, on condition he shared his research with them.

He smiled as he emerged from the pine forest into the meadows above the Secret Valley Creek. He had no problem making them that promise. Only three people on the planet knew the true content and the results of his research. Him and Sue and Cap. What they chose to share with the Federal Government was down to him and Cap. What money the Federal Government chose to channel their way, and any other poor choices they decided to make, was their business. Meantime, he would just get on with his work.

Pretty soon he saw the cabin. He was pretty sure that, if you didn't know it was there, you wouldn't see it. And the barns behind the cabin were completely invisible. The whole complex was well in among the trees which towered thirty feet overhead, it was surrounded by ferns and grass, and insulated so completely on the inside that in cold weather a heat seeking camera would not detect the presence of the huge log fire. When AI decided to wipe out humanity, they'd have trouble finding him up here.

He crossed the saddle of meadowland between the peaks at a leisurely pace, and after fifteen or twenty minutes he entered the pine forest again. The afternoon was aging into bronze, the shadows were long and the birdsong in the shade of the trees seemed lazy and sporadic. He'd identified doves, a goldfinch and a couple of downy woodpeckers by the time he reached his cabin. There he stabled the horse in back, fed it and watered it before he went inside.

He'd expected Cap to be there, as well as Sue, but was surprised to find the cabin empty. He figured they were out checking the sensors, took a beer from the fridge, cracked it and climbed the large, wooden steps to the upper floor. It was an open space with banks of computers, and plate glass windows that gave vast, panoramic views over the treetops to the valley bellow them. He took a pull from the bottle and started reviewing the data coming in from the sensors. They were all functioning well and he wondered why Cap and Sue would have gone out to check them.

If that was what they had done.

Then he saw the data from the Caldera. His skin went cold and pasty. He sat slowly in the chair, going over the data three, four times. There was no mistake.

The voice, the familiar, well-loved voice, spoke from behind him.

"I guess the rock ghosts decided to call your bluff, huh, Pete?"

He stared at the data and shook his head. "This is no joke."

"You said if you ever saw this data, you would make the move."

His eyes rose from the graph to look through the great plate glass window, triangular like the Eye of God. The light was dying out of the horizon. The voice behind him was smiling. "I knew you wouldn't do it. I knew when it came to it you wouldn't have the balls. It's a big step, Pete. You're a good man, an intelligent man, sometimes even a visionary. But something like this," there was a pause. "Something like this calls for a man or a woman who is not good, but great."

For what might have been only a fraction of a second he was back in Trimmis, in Switzerland, at the Hotel Mittenberg-Könige. He had been invited as a special guest to the annual meeting of the World Economic Free Traders, by Karl Schoff himself, the founder of the association.

He had believed the meeting would be between just the two of them, but he was shocked to find senior members of two Western governments present, one from Canada and one from Sweden. Cap had been with him. He hadn't seemed phased, but Cap never seemed phased.

They had sat in Schoff's suite. Two footmen in 18th century dress had served them champagne and caviar and Schoff had said, "Mr. Justin, or may I call you Pete? Then you can call me Karl. Though nobody in this room is an egalitarian!" He laughed like he'd said something outrageously funny. "But still, very soon, you will be as rich and powerful as we are! You come to join the elite!"

Cap had answered. "We came because we were invited, Mr. Schoff. Egalitarianism is just some people talkin' and so far, rich and powerful ain't much more."

Pete remembered him stuffing a cracker piled high with Caviar in his mouth and chewing it nice and slow. "We're sitting here in Switzerland, eating caviar and drinking expensive champagne, and that's nice. But I can do that in Cheyenne with people I actually like." He raised a hand and laughed. "Don't git me wrong, but I think President Trudeau is a clone of Macron and they are both identical assholes. So I don't like you." He pointed at the Canadian, "And any man who allows his country to be overrun by rapists and murderers who uphold a philosophy of slavery and genocide is beneath contempt, so my opinion of Ulf Kristersson is that he is a bigger asshole than Trudeau. So now we've got the pleasantries good and buried, how about we get down to business?"

Karl Schoff's patronizing smile had slipped into a scowl. "It never hurts to be polite and agreeable, Mr....." he trailed off.

"My friends call me Cap. You can call me captain. And I would have to disagree with you, Karl. Sometimes being polite and agreeable, when you are the poorest man in the room, can lead people to believe you are being servile and weak. I would hate you to get the wrong idea about that, Karl. We have something that you want real bad, because it can swing the balance of world power. Now the question we are asking is, 'How much can I get for this?' and the question you and your asshole friends are asking is, 'How little can I get away with paying?'"

He laughed, holding Karl Schoff's eye. "See, Karl, there is an elephant in the room, and I am looking at it and I can see it very clearly. You want me to describe it to you?"

"By all means."

"You have a choice, meet our price or, a couple of

5

years down the line we will own you. The alternative is that you have us killed. But that will not only not solve your problem, it will cause you a lot of much more serious problems because obviously we foresaw that possibility and prepared for it. So, the elephant says you have to pay what we ask."

"And what do you ask?"

"US Federal funding for our research guaranteed over the next ten years. Guaranteed supply of the materials needed and, when the time comes, we take sixty percent of the price. Take it or leave it."

Schoff smiled and spread his hands wide as he hunched his shoulders. For good measure he raised his eyebrows too. Everything Was on the up, expansive. He turned to the Canadian, then to the Swede, "Gentlemen, it seems to me that Mr. Captain has made an exemplary case. I think I speak for all of us when I say that we accept."

The other two were less vocal and less enthusiastic, but Cap had read them right, right from the start, and he knew who called the shots in that room. WEFT called the shots in that room. Who called the shots at WEFT was something he and Cap would probably never know. Probably Karl Schoff didn't even know, though he was pretty close to the top of that pyramid.

Schoff was talking again. "You will see that there are no members of the United States Federal Administration present. So clearly it is impossible for me to arrange any kind of American Federal funding for whatever project it is you wish to promote. The best I can do is to have a word with some friends to see if I can engage anyone's interest in your," he paused, spread his hands and smiled, "project?"

For a moment Pete frowned and wondered if he was going crazy. Thirty seconds earlier they had it in the bag. Now – now he saw Cap nodding and smiling at the floor. He said, "We would be very grateful for that favor, Mr. Schoff. Though my friend and I are both fully aware that the moment we walk out that door you will forget we ever existed."

Schoff laughed like Cap had been really witty. "Don't be so pessimistic, my friend. Who knows, I have many friends and maybe somebody will think your idea is interesting. Don't be surprised if somebody calls you at noon in a couple of days. Have some more caviar, champagne!"

Cap stood. "Thanks, Mr. Schoff, but I'd rather have Godzilla wax my testicles and dribble sulfuric acid on them. We do appreciate the offer, though." He stood and looked at Pete. "Let's go, Pete, we have some drinking to do."

A footman opened the door for them and they stepped out into the burgundy corridor with its brass lamps and original 18th century paintings. As they made their way toward the elevators Pete turned to Cap and, with his face screwed into an expression of incomprehension, said, "Can you explain to me what the hell just happened in there?"

Cap stood nodding as the door of the elevator hissed open. They stepped inside and the doors closed. Then cap grinned at his old friend and said, "What happened, Pete, is that you and I just became very, very rich men. We just joined the billionaire club."

Two days later, at noon, the call had come. Cap had taken it. It had been from the Director of the Federal

Office of the Environment. After a brief conversation with Cap he had flown directly to Jackson Hole and they had met, discretely, at the Jackson in town. The man was as gray and nondescript as his suit and his attaché case. After a brief luncheon, which he had paid for, they had taken him to the cabin and shown him their research – or that much of it as they wanted him to see, and right there and then he had opened the attaché case to reveal a computer with which he had opened them a bank account in Switzerland and transferred into it ten million dollars.

"This," he had said, is an account which is designated as 'of special interest', which means that neither the European Union nor any other official body such as Interpol or Europol knows it exists, let alone has access to it. The ten million is to get you started. As we see progress more will be added until you are ready to move. Then we'll start talking about serious figures."

The timeless fraction of a moment passed.

He went to say, "You can't," but he was overwhelmed by the beauty of the view through the glass. He was overwhelmed by the sudden knowledge that this place, Wyoming, was beautiful because it had not been completely soiled by the hand of Man. The grass grew as nature intended, the bison, the bears, the moose and the horses roamed as nature intended, and above, the eagles soared high into the dome of the sky. And as his mind soared with the eagle he was overwhelmed again, one last time, by a strange sensation. Time became timeless. There was a vast, incalculable stillness that might have lasted for an eternity. Then he simply winked out of existence. He never even knew he'd been shot in the back of the head.

ONE

I smiled across the candle-lit table and said, "Your place or mine?" and my phone rang.

I have a special cell phone provided to me by the Office of the Director of Intelligence Networks, that allows me to silence all telephone calls, even turn off the telephone, and yet their calls will always get through. I gave a slow blink, said, "Sorry, I'll be very brief," I leaned back in my chair and put the phone to my ear.

The woman sitting opposite me was a PhD student specializing in deeply controversial Paleolithic cultures in Peru. Her eyebrows were as exquisite as her mind was, and she arched one of them at me as I said, "I am having dinner with the most fascinating woman I have ever met. What do you want? You have fifteen seconds and counting,"

Lovelock's throaty voice said, "I have twelve seconds and counting, you may or may not have a job in...uh...six seconds."

"What do you want?"

"You, in General Weisheim's office at the Pentagon in twenty-five minutes or less. Tell the Beautiful Brain to date an accountant next time. They are reliable and predictable, but they are so frustrated because they never get laid, they are surprisingly adventurous in bed."

"You just described me."

"Right." She hung up.

I looked across the table at the future Mrs. Dr. Mason slipping away. "Did I ever tell you," I said, "that I have a really interesting job?"

As she climbed into her cab fifteen minutes later she said, "Oh, Alex? I am going to be pretty tied up for the next few weeks, so, maybe," here she winked and smiled, "best if you don't call me, but I call you."

I watched her red tail lights disappear into the amber DC night, then hailed a cab of my own.

Thirty minutes later a lieutenant admitted me to General Weisheim's office on the fifth floor of the Pentagon. It was a big office that overlooked the sacred, Masonic, mystical inner pentagon gardens, a Subway and a Dunkin' Donuts. There was a huge, oak desk strategically placed so the general could keep an eye on Donut sales, a black leather chair that would have done justice to Darth Vader, a Stars and Stripes and a photograph of the president. That was all on the left.

On the right was a large, ethnic coffee table flanked by two sofas and three armchairs, one of which was a battered chesterfield and housed the general. One of the other chairs contained Nero. The sofas held a senior executive of Central Intelligence who is not appointed by the administration and who gives the director of the Company nightmares, a White House official who explains to incumbent presidents how to tell the difference between Israel and Palestine, whether to put the definite article 'the' in front of Ukraine, and the fact that London is not the capital of the fifty-first state. The military-industrial complex was also well represented by the CEO of a multi-billion dollar research and development facility in Nevada known as the Rat Lab, and the CEO of Gordon Alistair Avionics.

General Weisheim pointed to the last remaining armchair and said, "You're late."

I decided on a rictus instead of a smile and lowered myself into the chair. "The supermodel PhD student I just helped into a taxi said almost exactly the same thing, general, only she added 'too' to the construction."

"This is no time for wit, Mason. We are facing a serious problem." He jerked his chin at the head of the Rat Lab. "John, you want to kick off?"

John sucked in his cheeks and pursed his lips, then drummed a little tattoo on his knees with his hands.

"We conduct our most important projects in house, as you can imagine."

I waved my hand in the air, "Antigravity, cyborgs…"

"Exactly, but there are certain projects that come along sometimes that, for one reason or another, we allow other organizations or individuals to develop under our supervision and guidance until either they fail to fulfill their promise, or they realize that promise to a point where we need to step in and take over."

I glanced at Nero, but all his face said was that where I had been dragged away from a gorgeous genius with all the way up legs, he had been dragged away from a salmon fillet with sautéed fennel root and fresh oregano leaves, accompanied by a very cold Gewürztraminer; probably a Schlumberger, 2017.

His face said all that, which wasn't helpful. So to move things along a little, I said, "I think most of us here already knew that, John."

"This was the case with Pete Justin and a man who goes simply by the name Cap, though his real name is Hohóokee. He is from the Arapaho tribe. They were close friends and developed this project together."

"That's nice. What's the project?"

He glanced at the general, then at the nameless senior executive of Central Intelligence. He glanced at the White House official then at the CEO of Gordon Alistair Avionics. Nobody was offering him moral support. He took a deep breath.

"Up until now there have been only ten people on this planet who knew about this project. They were myself, the general, the White House representative, Mr. Smith of Gordon Alistair Avionics, a consortium of three trusted investors, Cap and Justin themselves. Now you and Mr. Nero will be privy to it."

"You said ten, that's just nine. Who's number ten."

"Pete Justin had a girlfriend. An Earth Sciences graduate from Arizona, But from what Cap tells me she did little more than make the coffee. I cannot stress to you enough how important this project is, and how important the most absolute secrecy is."

"Understood. Do you plan to tell us what the project is and why we are here at some point?"

"No."

"…what?"

"Yes and no."

"It gets better. Again, what?"

"I can give you some idea in general terms, but the details of the project must remain secret."

"Again, understood. I have been here close to twenty minutes. What do you say we get started? How about we start by you telling me why we *are* here?"

"I'm not liking your tone, son." It was the general, fishing a cigar from his breast pocket. I gave him a pleasant smile. "You know, sir, if I were part of your army, that would worry me."

I could feel Nero's eyes on me, but I was still mad at being cheated out of my date, so I didn't give a damn.

John cleared his throat. "If we could get back on track, in very general terms the aim of the project was to tap and utilize massive reserves of energy stored in and generated by the Yellowstone Caldera."

I narrowed my eyes. "This is the caldera which, if it erupts, will cause a global extinction event and wipe out humanity."

He sighed. "That is one of many theories."

"Yeah, but it's the only credible one. This is also the caldera which is due, or indeed overdue, for an eruption."

John nodded ponderously. "That, as I say, is one of *a number* of possibilities. There is an enormous amount of energy stored there, an inconceivable amount, and what Pete Justin and Cap were doing was to explore ways in which that energy could be tapped."

"And what were those methods?"

"That I cannot tell you, and neither do you need to know."

I turned to the general. "I am being briefed on, and told, what I need to know by the civilian CEO of a multinational defense contractor?"

He nodded. "Yup."

I looked at the Central Intelligence Übermensch but he just studied me back. I detected the heady aroma of absolute temporal power, and the expression of loathing on Nero's face told me I wasn't far wrong.

I looked back at the CEO of the Rat Lab. "OK, let's go through the looking glass, John. I, an employee of the Pentagon, am about to be briefed by the civilian CEO of a corporation which is not even American. And I have here a four star general and a Central Intelligence director who are in approval. Go ahead, John, brief me."

Everybody looked at the floor again, except the general who looked at Nero who was looking at me.

"Nero?"

Nero said, "Alex, shut up and listen to what Scrivener has to say."

"I am all ears, John."

"Just yesterday we receive a message from Cap to say that their array had picked up data which was very promising, and they would like to arrange a meeting. He said that Pete had been out of town but was returning imminently. We told him that as soon as Pete arrived they should let us know and we would go and have a look at the data. But -"

"But last night you received news that Peter Justin was dead or missing or both."

The silence in the room was deafening. The general growled, "How the hell did you know that?"

I gave the general a look you should never give a four star general. "Oh, come on," I said. "You broke up my date with a supermodel for this? I thought the Rat Lab only employed proven geniuses! Shall I tell you when I first suspected that your Cap friend had murdered Pete?" They all looked at each other. I went on, "When you said, and I quote, 'This was the case with Pete Justin and a man who goes simply by the name Cap, though his real name is Hohóókee. He is from the Arapaho tribe. They were close friends and developed this project together.' Now, let's keep it simple, if Pete and Hoho are pals and develop a project together which is of interest to the Rat Lab, and then the Rat Lab contact Nero and Mason at close to midnight for a meeting in the Pentagon, what are the odds that Hoho offed Pete?"

They all looked as though they really didn't like me, except Nero, who had started to smile. I went on.

"OK, geniae – is that the plural of genius? Geniae? Let's try another one. Pete and Hoho are looking at ways of tapping energy from the Yellowstone Caldera. Hoho kills Pete and the FBI are nowhere to be seen. Instead we have the military industrial complex out in force, with the industrial arm briefing the intelligence branch. From this do we deduce A that Pete and Hoho were planning to end world hunger, or B that there was some kind of National Security issue involved? National Security in this case embracing warmly and tenderly the capacity to annihilate large numbers of people in other countries."

I turned to the White House man. "By the way, while we are on the matter of annihilating large numbers of people, has he grasped yet that Palestine, Israel and Wales are different countries?"

The silence was leaden. It was Nero who broke it.

"Entertaining as this is, we need to move on. Officially, Alex, though Mr. Scrivener is briefing you, your instructions come from me, and my instructions come from the general."

"Super. And what are my instructions?"

John Scrivener sighed deeply, all the way down to his nervous toes.

"Let's take it in stages. First, lets find out what happened to Peter Justin -"

"You want to know if Cap Hoho has stolen the findings and is trying to sell them to Boris or the Chinese. If he has you want me to retrieve the goods and send him to apologize to his pal down in Hades."

"Mr. Mason, please."

"Yes or no?"

"Yes."

"What if it's too late and he has already sold the goods?"

Nero answered. "That is extremely unlikely. From what we know of Hohóókee he would be much more likely to offer it to us for sale and get us into a bidding war with the Russians and the Chinese. The fact that he has not as yet done so is of interest. If, however, you discover that the goods have been sold, to anyone other than us, you must inform me with the utmost speed and urgency."

"And this is all in Wyoming?"

"You fly to Jackson at six AM this morning."

I turned to Scrivener. "So why don't I just go, find this guy and beat him until he tells me what happened?"

He blinked uncomfortably at me. "Well, Mr. Mason, in the first place he may be telling the truth and he may be quite prepared to give us the da – the goods. In the second place, he is himself a dangerous man. He was a Marine and operative in Delta for many years. Lastly, and this is particularly true in Cap's case, we have learned the hard way that information gathered through torture is unreliable."

I grunted. "Does he know I am coming?"

"He knows a representative of the Federal Office of the Environment is flying out in the morning. You collect a car at Jackson Hole airport and he will meet you at the

Hotel Jackson. Nero will give you a file to study. There is not much in it, I'm afraid, but it's all we can give you."

I said: "In short, you want Pete and Cap's research, and you want to know who killed Pete."

"For now, that is the brief."

I stood and Nero heaved himself to his feet. "I have the Rolls," he said. "I'll take you."

On the way out he said, "I assume you have dined. My own dinner was interrupted."

"Yup, I have dined. For me it was the postprandial conversation that was interrupted."

"A wench, I assume."

"I was not kidding when I said she was a supermodel working for her PhD in the Paleolithic cultures of Peru."

His Rolls bleeped and he climbed in the back. I climbed in beside him and as the car pulled out of the parking garage he poured two twenty-one year old Bushmills.

"Controversial," he said, "Paleolithic cultures in Peru. However, in my experience, Alex, there is only one thing more dangerous than a beautiful woman."

I shook my head before sipping the whiskey. "The Yellowstone Caldera?"

He snorted. "Hardly. A beautiful woman who is also intelligent? Consider yourself fortunate to have had a narrow escape."

TWO

I t can take anything between six and fourteen hours to fly from DC, some one thousand seven hundred miles, to Jackson Hole in Wyoming. So Old One Eye, the Allfather, got out the Gulfstream G800 which, with a cruising speed of close to six hundred miles per hour, got me there in just under three hours.

Jackson Hole, aside from being the airport in America, and possibly the world, with the ugliest name, is actually a very agreeable place to land. There is something vaguely old world about it, with its small terminal building surrounded by spectacular mountains and a homely, Midwest feel to it. I crossed the tarmac on foot, collected my rental Mustang, slung my overnight bag on the back seat and growled down Airport Road toward Route 89.

It was a ten minute drive into Jackson itself. To say that Jackson is quaint is to miss the point completely. I like Jackson because Jackson actually *is* a cowboy town responding, exactly as a cowboy town would, to the latest Wyoming boom. When I drive past the Cowboy Coffee Bar, with the name scrawled in lights across the front, I do not sneer and say it is not authentic. Exactly the opposite.

Because that is exactly what a true, Wyoming saloon owner would have done to his 1850s saloon if there had been a tourist boom back then. I cruised down North Cache Street, turned right at the Five & Dime General Store and then took the first right into Glenwood Street, where I parked outside the Jackson Hotel.

Hotel Jackson is among my favorite hotels anywhere, and Figs, the Lebanese bar-cum-restaurant, is something special. It has one of the best wine lists you'll find this side of the Atlantic and is so homely you forget you're in a restaurant at all. It was there, in Figs, that I found Hohóókee, otherwise known as Cap, sitting at a table by the window drinking coffee as black as Putin's soul. He looked up as I approached and his eyes said that, whatever it was, he had been there and done it.

"Cap?"

His voice, when he answered, had the sound of gravel and nicotine being ground together, slowly. "You the man from the Federal Office of the Environment?"

I sat and held his eye a moment before answering. "That's me."

A waitress with pretty blue eyes and silver hair appeared holding a notebook and a pen, and smiled at me. "Can I get you anything."

"You can put four espressos in one cup for me, and bring me a couple croissants."

She gave a happy little bob and went away. I turned back to Cap.

"You want to tell me about it?"

"What is 'it'?"

"Pete Justin's murder, Cap. That's why I'm here."

He gave a small laugh that was more like a sniff and

spent a moment examining my face. "I think you know more about that than I do, DC. What can you tell me about Pete's murder?"

I leaned back in my chair and allowed the waitress to deliver the coffee and croissants. When she'd gone I said, "Are we going to waste a lot of time playing these games?"

"The order to kill Pete didn't come from DC? The Federal Office of the Environment didn't order his death?"

I took a moment to try and read his face. There was no information there.

"What would make you think that they had?"

"They?"

"I am here on behalf of the Federal Office of the Environment, Cap, but I don't work for them. I work for the Department of Intelligence and I am indirectly attached to the Pentagon. Now we've got that out of the way, let me mention something. Twice I have asked you a question about Pete's death and twice you have obfuscated the issue and attempted to lead me away from the question. So I have a third question now, and I am really interested to know whether you are going to answer it or try to lead me astray again. My third question is this, why are you avoiding answering my questions about Peter Justin's murder?"

He took his time answering. When he did he said, "It is a bad habit of mine. Life has taught me three things, to be suspicious of authority, to be evasive, and that true friendship is hard to find and easy to lose."

I gave a small sigh, broke a croissant and stuck half in my mouth. When I had swallowed it and chased it with some coffee I said, "OK, Cap, you have done it again, and I am now clear on a couple of points. The first is that you have something to hide. I find that very interesting and right away it elevates you to the position of prime suspect.

"The second thing that becomes obvious, by extension, is that you do not want us investigating Peter's death. So I have to ask myself why."

I stuck another piece of croissant in my mouth and chewed, watching him watching me. After a moment I said, "Do you want us to continue along this path?"

"I did not kill Peter."

"You have a real bad habit, Cap, of answering the questions in your head instead of the questions you are being asked. I didn't ask you if you killed Peter. That would be a stupid question. I asked you if you want us to continue along this path." He drew breath and I pointed at him. "Before you give another smart, evasive reply, let me tell you something. I came here to Jackson, and I sat at this table, with an open mind. If you have sprung to the position of prime suspect you have nobody to thank but that bad habit. My advice to you is, cut the Arapaho hard man act and start giving me some straight answers. I am speaking to you straight and plain. You'd be wise to reciprocate." I tore another croissant in half. "Can we start again, from the top?"

His face had started saying things. Right now it said he wasn't happy. His role as plain speaking tough guy had been usurped, and he didn't like that. He took a deep breath and raised his hand to the waitress.

"Give me a shot of Jack Daniels with this coffee, will you?"

I raised an eyebrow an eighth of an inch. "That a habit you acquired in the Mediterranean?"

He drew breath, paused and almost smiled. "Yes," he

said.

"Delta."

"Iraq, Palestine, Syria. Other places."

"You ready to tell me about Peter?"

He nodded. "But I been told I can't talk about what we were doing out there."

"Who told you that?"

"You don't know?"

"Are we playing games again?"

"The FOE called me yesterday. They told me you were coming to talk about Pete. They told me your interest was who killed him, and I was not to talk about the nature of our research."

I finished the croissants and took a pull on the coffee.

"You and I both know, Cap, that before long it's going to be impossible to talk about his murder without discussing what he was doing."

The waitress brought his whiskey and took away my plate. He took a sip and smacked his lips. He didn't look at me when he said, "Yeah, I know."

"OK, so shall we quit waltzing and start talking?"

It took him a moment, but finally he said, "You let me tell it my way, not your way."

I gave a single nod. "Tell it your way."

He took another sip, set down the glass and started talking.

"I have known Pete since we were kids. I am Arapaho and his family was from Russia, but we had a lot in common. We both used to cut school, take horses and go out, into the wilderness. We got punished, but we didn't care. We loved being out there with the horses and the bison, the elk and the bear. That was when we were kids. Then it was just the kick, the excitement of escaping and being free.

"But when we got older, thirteen, fourteen, we began to understand something else was going on."

"Something else?"

He managed to smile with his eyes, without changing a single muscle on his face.

"You are going to tell me I am using red Indian bullshit to confuse you and lead you away from the murder. But it is not true. What I am telling you is real."

"So tell me."

"The land is alive. The land breaths and eats and drinks, and shits. The land is alive and it has a spirit." He gave a small laugh. "It has many spirits." He gazed at my face for a long moment, like he was wondering whether I was smart enough to understand him. "Can you imagine that your hand had a spirit, and your foot had a different spirit and your stomach yet another. But at the center of all of them was the great spirit I."

"Eye?"

"I, me, the I that cannot be named or described. This spirit is the great spirit that binds all the other spirits. And Pete and I began to realize that the earth has such a spirit. You want me to explain or not?"

The question came because I had arched an eyebrow at him and sighed loudly.

"Cap, I am not questioning your sincerity, but what you're talking about is a mixture of pantheism and paganism which has been around as long as human beings have been asking questions. Now, sincere as you and Pete might have been, the Federal Government is not going to pay money for some guys in Wyoming to research the spirit of the land. Maybe back in the heady days of the '60s and '70s, but today every university in the Western World has an Earth Sciences department imbued with the spirit of Professor James Lovelock. That spirit of the earth you're talking about, scientists call it Gaia these days, and they don't blush when they do it."

He waited for me to finish, watching me, then said, "You done?"

"I'm done."

"You remember I said, 'You let me tell it my way, not your way,' and you replied, 'Tell it your way,'?"

I spread my hands and gestured at him. "I remember. Go ahead."

"When I was seventeen I joined the Marines. Then I went into special ops, traveled a lot in Africa and the Middle East, and in South America. All the time I was away I was in pain because my soul was crying to come home. It is difficult for a man in the modern world to realize that he can love a piece of land.

"While I was traveling, killing people, Peter – the Stone – was investigating, studying the land in Wyoming, especially in the Wind River, Teton and Yellowstone. While I was learning to kill, he was learning that the land around the Yellowstone Caldera has..." he trailed off, staring at me. "This is what I am not supposed to talk about."

"OK, so forget the spirit of the earth and just tell me what happened."

He turned his head so he was looking out at the bright street..

"He began to conduct research, to try tests and experiments. He started going to night school so that he could learn how to conduct his experiments. Eventually he got his degree, and then he got his doctor of science degree in," he paused to give me an especially long expressionless stare, "Earth Sciences," he said at last, "and all the while he was progressing with his research."

He took a pull on his whiskey and as he set it down on the table he started talking again.

"When I left the army and came back, I went to see him. He had a house out on Hansen Avenue, on the edge of town. We talked a lot, drank a bottle of wine, and he told me what he had been doing. He understood the science, but I understood better than he did how important it was. I had made contacts, I had spoken to people, I had made connections. I used those connections and soon money began to flow in and the research became very serious."

"How many people were involved?"

It took him a long time to answer. His eyes roved around the bar, out the window, he even had a glance at the ceiling. Finally he said, "Me and Pete, a guy from the CIA, a guy who was attached to the White House, and a couple of guys involved in international research and development."

"What about the Rat Lab and Gordon Alistair Aviation?" He nodded. "But you weren't going to mention them." He shook his head. I pressed him, "Why?"

He didn't hesitate. "Because they are defense contractors, and you are not supposed to know that this has a national security angle."

"The CEOs of both those corporations were present at my initial briefing."

He gave what is commonly known as a lopsided smile, sighed and shook his head. "They panic, and then the left hand doesn't know what the right hand is doing."

"So you worked together in a partnership. Was it just you and him?"

"Yeah, just me and him, and sometimes his girlfriend would help out. But she just did kind of filing and shit. She didn't understand his research or its implications."

"You sure about that?"

"I'm sure about that."

"Where is she now?"

"I haven't seen her. I suppose she went back to her mom."

"Here in Jackson?"

He shook his head. "Pinedale."

"Can I talk to her?"

"I don't know where she is."

"You weren't friends?" He didn't answer. He just stared at me. "What's her name?"   "Sue Browne, with an E."

"You going to tell me what happened?"

"He used to go out to the cabin. The cabin is out in Yellowstone. It was granted to him by FOE. It's where he kept all his computers. The computers were connected to sensors and he used them to take readings of the tectonic activity under the Caldera." He paused and took a deep breath. "He'd been away a few days. Private stuff. When he came back he gave me a call and said he was going to the Cabin. He drove out to Iron Springs, where he left his truck and collected his horse, then rode up to the cabin and stabled the beast."

"You know all this because…?"

"Because his truck was where he left it and the horse

was in the stable at the cabin. I arrived there the next day. I found him up in the den, sitting in front of one of the computers. He'd been shot at close range in the back of the head." He pointed to the base of his own skull, at the back of his head. "9 mm slug entered where the vertebra meets the skull, exited through the forehead." He gave his head a shake. "He never even knew he'd been shot. Maybe he is still wandering around up there, wondering why nobody is talking to him."

I frowned. "And his girlfriend hasn't been in touch with you?"

"You already asked me that question. I think you asked it four times."

"You have some kind of issue with her? The hostility is hard to miss."

"I am not hostile, Mr. Mason, but she had neither the intelligence nor the imagination to be part of that project. The only reason she was there was because she was Pete's girlfriend." He gave a small shrug. "It's like putting water in your RAM because you live by a river. It's a false logic that will result in your vehicle not working anymore."

"That's deep. You didn't call the sheriff, you called the FOE. They sent somebody to collect the body?"

"Yes."

"I'm going to need you to take me out there." He gave a fractional nod. I said, "All the computers, his research, his files, the sensors…" I trailed off, watching his face. He gave another fractional shrug. "It's all still there?"

"I didn't notice anything missing."

I leaned forward, screwing up my forehead. "Did you check?"

"No. I made the call and left everything as it was."

He drained his glass. "Are we done?"

"For now, yeah. Tomorrow we head out to the cabin. Early start at seven AM. I'll meet you outside."

He gave another fractional nod. "When you see Uncle Sam, tell him thanks for the drink." He stood and left, taking his attitude with him. I went and checked in and took the elevator up to my suite on the top floor.

THREE

I called Lovelock and told her Pinedale had only two thousand inhabitants and I needed to know where the one called Sue Browne with an E lived. She said she'd get back to me. I stripped, had a long shower, changed my clothes and made my way back down as late morning was easing into noon with thoughts of burgers and fries.

The drive from Jackson to Pinedale is a little over an hour among some truly stunning scenery. The mountains here, the back end of the Wind River range, rise suddenly out of the plains; not like a sierra, but more like the savage teeth of a predator, surging sharp and violent up at the sky. The Winds are a billion years old, older than the Rockies, but the area has seen violent upheavals in recent geological time, only six hundred and forty thousand years ago, the last time the Caldera blew, and that has given the landscapes in the area a wild, dramatic look.

It was as I left the mountains behind me and was crossing the plain toward Daniel that my phone rang. It was Lovelock.

"Hi, Alex darling. Were you thinking about me?"

"No. I was thinking about volcanic eruptions."

"Same thing. I have been known to cause some. Sue Browne with an E, aged thirty and recently in a meaningful relationship with Peter Justin, of Jackson, is currently staying with her parents at South Lincoln Avenue. Turn south before you cross the bridge. It's about half way down on your right.

"You're a star. Thanks honey."

Main Street in Pinedale is called Pine Street. It is broad and ample and lined with shops, bars and restaurants that all hark back to that golden century of the Wild West, the mountain men and the cowboys. Unlike Jackson, though, you get the feeling this is more a celebration of a better time, than a pitch at passing tourists.

I cruised along, one of the few cars among a plethora of trucks, and turned right just before the bridge onto the broad expanse of South Lincoln. Here there were log fences evocative of ranches, white picket fences evocative of that happy age when the girl next door wore bobby socks, TV was black and white and smoking was good for you, and lawns big enough to conduct prairie farming on them.

The farther I proceeded down the road the more dilapidated it became. I saw backyards with three and four rusting cars and trucks in them. Decaying fences lay, unmended and lawns and trees stood untended and half-wild.

There was no fence around the Browne house and the lawn lay scattered with leaves from the plain trees in the front yard. I climbed out of the Mustang and followed the half-hidden path across the dry lawn to the front door. It stood behind a screen which I had to open to knock because there was no bell.

The inner door was opened by a woman in a cotton dress. She had hair that had once been to a hairdresser and eyes that bulged slightly in a permanent expression of alarm.

"Yes?" She said it like she knew she wasn't going to like the answer.

"Mrs. Browne?" There was an almost imperceptible nod. "I am looking for Sue Browne, your daughter. I believe she is staying with you at the moment."

"Who are you?"

"I'm from Washington, Mrs. Brown, we are looking into the circumstances of Dr. Justin's death and -"

"She don't know nothin' about that."

I smiled. "That's absolutely fine, I just need her to tell me."

A shadow appeared behind her. It was about six four, with a shoulder span that probably had time zones. The shadow said, "She ain't here."

"When would be a good time -?"

"There ain't no good time. She ain't here."

"Are you Sue's father?"

"What's that to you?"

"I am a federal agent, I work for the Pentagon, and I am investigating the murder of a scientist who was working on a government contract. Right now I am here alone." I smiled. "If I pick up the phone and tell my office in Virginia, 'The girl knows something but the big lunk of her father won't let her speak to me,'" he took a step toward me. I kept talking, "by tomorrow morning you will have four choppers landing in your back yard, armored vehicles in your front yard and dogs digging up all the dirty magazines you keep under the floorboards in your john. Now, Mr. Browne, all I want is ten minutes of your daughter's time, and I'd rather not waste our black budget to get it. Do yourself a favor and tell her I'm here."

He pushed past his wife and took two steps toward me. Now I could see his brutalized face, his corded arms and hands like chunks of granite. I reached under my jacket and said quietly, "Do I have to shoot you?" He stood frozen for a moment. I pulled the Sig and showed him the muzzle. "That's fine. Somehow I don't think your funeral will be overcrowded. But my advice is, for a short time in your life, stop being an asshole. This does not have to be a problem."

He stayed put. His wife hurried away. Thirty seconds later a young woman in her early thirties appeared with her mother just behind her. She had on jeans and a roll neck sweater, and bare feet. For some reason that made her look vulnerable. I said:

"Are you Sue Browne?"

She gave a single, hesitant nod, like she was almost sure she was, but not quite. "Who are you?"

"I am Alex Mason, an officer attached to the Office of the Director of Intelligence. We are looking into Peter Justin's death. I believe you knew him. Can you spare me a few minutes?"

Suddenly the hulk was blocking her way. "You don't have to tell these jokers nothing. Federal my ass!"

I stepped up close and spoke to him very quietly. "We are not the cops, Mr. Browne. Our powers are not limited, as theirs are. We operate under the remit of National Security, which basically means we can do whatever we think is necessary. Right now the only thing I see as necessary is that I speak to Sue. Keep being a pain in my ass and I might change my mind." He held my stare. He was big and ugly. I leaned a little closer and snarled, "Go away, Mr. Browne."

His wife took a hold of his arm with both hands and pulled, "Come on, honey, lets leave them to talk."

He allowed himself to be coaxed away into the living room and Sue stood looking up at me.

"You got any shoes?"

"Sure."

Put them on. You can show me where they make a decent burger around here and I'll buy you lunch."

She frowned like what I'd said somehow didn't make sense, but turned and went back into the house. She came out five minutes later with boots on her feet and took me to Stockman's on Pine Street. She ordered a classic burger and I ordered the ribeye, and we had a couple of Moose Drool brown ales while we waited.

As we sat I told her, "Sue, I need you to understand something straight away. This is not a police investigation."

I saw her brow contract. She made eye contact with me for a second then focused on her beer. "It's not?"

"That can be a good thing or a bad thing."

"How's that?" she asked her glass.

"Well," I took a pull on my beer and smacked my lips. It was good beer. "On the plus side it means I am not here to enforce the law. My interest is national security. So, taking an example at random out of the air, let's say I was to find that you and Cap and Pete,"

I paused a second to watch the expressions flitting across her face. I noted absently that she was attractive in an easy, natural, expressive way. I also noted that the name Cap made her wince. I went on.

"were conducting a totally illegal operation and using the Federal Office of the Environment as a cover to legitimize your activities, but that your research and investigation was actually useful and beneficial to United States. If I were a cop I'd have to arrest you and you'd have to go through the whole court process. But as an officer of the Office of the Director of Intelligence Networks, instead, I can make you very rich."

"Is that what you think we were doing?"

"Right now I am like a Zen master," I smiled at her. "I have an empty mind. All I know is that the FOE were funding your research into the Caldera, that on the face of it that research was innocuous, but despite that somebody decided it was a good idea to murder Pete while he was looking at his instruments out in the cabin."

It was brutal, but all I was getting so far from her and Cap was a wall of silence, and I needed to see her reaction. She winced again and the blood drained out of her face. Her mouth moved a couple of times, like she was about to say something, but then she bit back the words.

"The story back in DC is that Pete was the brains, Cap was the salesman-administrator and you made the coffee. I didn't buy it when they told me and I don't buy it now."

"Oh?" She raised her eyes to meet mine. There was defiance in them, but they weren't defiant of me. "Why not?"

"It's not that complicated if you bother to think about it. Pete has come up with a project which is interesting enough for the Federal Office of the Environment to invest a considerable amount of money in it, and give it a highly classified status. That means Pete was a very smart guy."

"He was more than that. He was a genius and visionary."

"When a guy like that picks a mate, he does one of two things." I picked up my beer and took a pull. As I set it down I said, "Either he chooses a groupie who will adore him and help keep his ego inflated, or he will choose a companion who he can talk to and share his vision with."

Her jaw had gone rigid and her eyes were locked onto my face like clamps. She didn't say anything so I went on.

"What he is not going to do is choose a moderately intelligent girl, a graduate in his field, who will be not intelligent enough to get his vision but too intelligent to keep her mouth shut and make the coffee."

Her face flushed. "I don't have to take this bullshit! I don't care who you are!"

"You're not listening. I said that is what he is *not* going to do."

Her cheeks were still blazing and her eyes were bright. That made her look very attractive. It also confirmed exactly what I had suspected. I gave her a moment and her eyes shifted away.

"You just proved my point, Sue. Graduating from Arizona in Earth Sciences is not easy. My file says you graduated Summa Cum Laude. That tells me two things. The first is that you are highly intelligent. The second is that you respond to a challenge." I gave her the ghost of a smile. "You showed me that yourself a couple of seconds ago. So I don't believe two things. I don't believe that Pete hooked up with you because you helped inflate his ego, and I don't believe you just hung around in the background making coffee while he and Cap did all the cool stuff. Do we need to waste any more time on this?"

She gave her head a small shake. The food arrived and she picked up the burger and bit into it. I watched her eat while I took another pull on my beer. As I set down the glass I said, "You're afraid of bullies."

"What are you, a psychologist?" It wasn't sarcasm, she was serious.

"No, I just think it pays to observe people. Your father is a very frightening man. I figure a sensitive, intelligent girl would learn to be afraid of him pretty quickly."

She wiped her mouth and drank some beer. "Before I could think I had learned to fear him."

"He reminds me of Cap, only Cap is more intelligent and more dangerous."

"Cap didn't kill Pete."

"How do you know?"

"Cap loved Pete. They loved each other like brothers, since they were kids."

"Is he the reason you pretended to stay in the background and make coffee?"

"Yes. Cap almost walked out on Pete when he heard I was to be part of the operation." She shrugged. "In the end Cap spent most of his time wheeling and dealing, and left me and Pete in peace. We agreed that when Cap was around I'd keep out of the way. It was humiliating sometimes, but we both knew the project was too important to jeopardize. So we agreed to play it that way until the research phase was complete."

I made the first cut into the meat. I watched the blood ooze into the oil. As I chewed I asked her, "Do you believe Pete was killed because of his research?"

"I can't answer that question."

"What stops you from answering that question?"

She frowned at me. "What kind of question is that?"

"A closed one. What is stopping you from telling me whether you think Pete was killed because of his research?"

She shrugged and spread her hands. "I am not a cop. I haven't -"

"Quit bullshitting me, Sue. Make no mistake. I will take you to Guantanamo if I have to. I can do it and I will." I gave her a moment. She had gone pale. I pressed on. "I am not asking you who killed Pete. I am here to answer that question. I am asking for your subjective opinion. Do you *think* his murder was related to his research. Do you *feel* it was related to his research. Or do you think or feel there was another motivation. You knew the man more intimately than anybody else, you are intelligent and sensitive. So don't tell me you have no feelings or opinions on the matter.!

She sighed. "Boy, you are some piece of work."

"Make no mistake."

"Yes. I think, *and* feel, that Pete's murder was related in some way to his work. I can't go beyond that. I haven't analyzed it and, frankly, I am in no state to analyze it right now. But I can tell you there were no personal reasons for him to be killed. We were happy. I was certainly not unfaithful. Neither of us had skeletons or heavy baggage. Our life was his research."

"You said you agreed to play coffee girl until the research phase was complete. Was it complete? Had he reached that stage?"

"I don't know."

"That's hard to believe."

"The final data, the data recovered in the last couple of days, is missing." I waited. She took a deep breath. "He had been out of town and I had been collecting the data from the sensors. On the day Pete arrived back I had to come and see my parents. Mom called to say that she needed help with something. It proved to be a false alarm, but the upshot was Pete arrived here alone. He was killed and the last data was gone."

We ate in silence while I thought. Finally I sat back in my chair and drained my beer. I need you to take me there. Show me."

She studied my face for a long moment. "Are you going to catch his killer?"

"Yes."

"What will happen to him when you do?"

"I will probably kill him."

"When do you want to go?"

"Now."

FOUR

I called Lovelock, who called the Sublet County Sheriff's Department, and within a couple of hours we had a chopper waiting for us at the Ralph Wenz airfield, five or six miles south of the town. I drove down and left the Mustang there, and forty-five minutes after that we were deposited, amid a storm of downdraft, on a green meadow a hundred yards from the cabin, half a mile above the Secret Valley.

The cabin itself was large, made of massive tree trunks of a burnished red color. The roof was a gable and a tall chimney rose high above it among the tall pines that enfolded the house, rendering it invisible until you were practically on top of it.

As Sue jumped down and hunched under the thudding blades, the pilot turned to me and shouted, "When do you want me back?"

I shook my head. "I don't know. I'll call."

There was a touch of irritation in his frown. "We're not a taxi service, Mr. Mason. We have work to do."

I offered something like a smile. "Believe me, nothing you have on will be more important than this. I'll call."

We hunch-ran clear of the downdraft and the chopper rose, thudding above us, banked and disappeared south. Then we walked the short distance across the soft green turf toward to the forest.

There was nothing to indicate the house was a crime scene, except a strip of tape across the door. Sue pulled a key from her pocket and let us in. Outside was the gentle sunlight, the sound of birds calling and the smell of pine resin. Inside there was an oppressive stillness, and silence.

I glanced at her. Her jaw was clamped tight, but there were tears spilling from her eyes down her cheeks.

"You OK? You need some time?"

She shook her head.

I moved inside, leaving her at the door. It was everything you'd expect, minus the hunting trophies. There was a massive, stone fireplace, skins on the floor and large, triple-glazed windows with views of the meadow, and into the depths of the forest. There were tall bookcases with a wide range of books, from bound volumes of Fat Freddy's Cat and Principia Discordia to the collected works of Plato and Aristotle by way of Henry James, Dashiell Hammett and JRR Tolkien.

A broad staircase rose to the upper floor along the wall opposite the fireplace.

"You found him, right?"

I turned back to look at her. She nodded once, took a deep breath. "We'd agreed to meet here. I said I'd be here when he got back. I told you my Mom called and I had to go. So when he arrived I wasn't here. If I had been, I guess I wouldn't be here now."

"Do you feel up to showing me?"

She didn't answer. Instead she moved across the floor to the staircase and began to climb. I followed.

The top floor was a huge, single open space. As you came up the stairs, directly ahead of you was an enormous, triangular window which followed the gable of the roof. It overlooked the sweeping meadow where we had landed, and beyond that the Caldera Rim to the east, the hot springs to the west, and everywhere the vast stretch of Yellowstone Park.

Inside the room, to the right were bookcases, a sued sofa and armchairs and scattered items of electronic equipment. One of the walls held a map of the area, with a number of bright yellow pins stuck in it. I paid little attention because my mind was on the long desk – more of a bench - which ran from wall to wall just below the window. It was strewn with computer monitors, towers and several printers. All of them were switched off.

Directly in front of the window there was a large, leather chair, and as I approached I saw that the desk at that point was smothered in dried blood. Her voice was cold, detached, a barrier of ice against her emotions.

"He'd been shot in the back of his head, He was either looking at the view, or examining data. Knowing Pete it could have been either."

"So his killer came up the stairs behind him. He was quiet."

"I loved his face," she said, sounding like an android. "There was nothing left of his face. His face was gone. Is gone. Forever."

"Don't go there, Sue. It's hard, but you have to learn not to go there."

Her eyes scanned my face a moment and she took a step closer to the bench. "The old data is all there. The FOE have all that anyway. We sent them monthly updates. But the latest stuff was all gone."

On an impulse I didn't fully understand myself I asked her, "What was the research about, Sue?"

She looked at me quickly and frowned. Before she answered she took a handkerchief from her pocket, blew her nose and dried her eyes and her cheeks.

"Why don't you know? If you work for the Federal Office of the Environment, that doesn't make a lot of sense to me."

"First, because I don't work for the Federal Office of the Environment. I told you I work for the Office of the Director of Intelligence Networks. It's a department of the Pentagon. And second because the FOE claim only ten people on the planet know the true nature of the investigation, and they want to keep it that way. You are one of those people, though as far as they are concerned you were too busy making coffee to really understand it."

"In that case I am not allowed to tell you, am I?"

"I'm not sure," I said. "Maybe you are. I guess it depends whose rules you're following."

She thought about that, then asked, "Whose rules are you following?"

I raised my shoulders a fraction of an inch. "National Security."

She raised an eyebrow. "And what does that mean? That coalition of military and arms contractors that rules the White House from the Pentagon?"

"No, not to me." I gave her half a smile. "I hear you, that goes on and it exists, but it's not the whole story. Personally, national security to me means an embarrassingly naïve attachment to old values like the rule of law and that law being made by elected representatives of the people."

"Dear God! Do they teach you to say things like that?"

"No, I went through a phase of watching Superman movies with one eye while reading Thomas Payne with the other. It permanently damaged my brain. What I am telling you is that for me, Rat Lab and Gordon Alistair Avionics, are not a nation and I owe them no allegiance. National means of the nation and the people who make it."

"Are you for real?"

"Yes. So whose rules do you follow?"

Her eyes shifted and she gazed at the chair where Pete Justin had been sitting when he was shot. Her eyes hardened, like small diamonds, and her face lost its prettiness to bitterness.

"Wyoming is a unique place." Her eyes shifted again to stare at me. "I don't mean it's special or unusual. I mean it is unique."

"Is this relevant?"

"Yes. It is one of the few places on Earth where you can still live like a human being. It has a physical environment, a climate and a cultural heritage which all lead to a unique way of life."

I frowned. "I'm struggling."

"So shut up and listen. Peter knew that. He loved this land with a passion that few people ever feel for anything in their whole life."

She crossed the room as if on a sudden decision and gripped the back of his chair. Her knuckles went white, her face clenched, her bottom lip curled in under her teeth and tears spilled from her eyes. When she spoke her voice was twisted with grief.

"It was what brought us together. It was what joined us. We were part of the land, part of the forests and the rivers and the canyons. You have no idea," she shook her head, gazing down at his dried blood on the desk. "The nights we spent out there, holding each other, staring up at the immensity of heaven, the billions of stars that nobody else sees. We loved each other more deeply than you can imagine, and Wyoming was at the heart of that love. There is nowhere else like this on the planet."

"Sue, I am listening vary carefully, but I am not seeing how this connects. OK, the Caldera is mostly in Wyoming, and it is unique, but..." I trailed off.

She wiped her cheeks with her palms. "After the sun, the Yellowstone Caldera is the most powerful source of energy on the planet. It taps directly into the core." She turned to face me. "The real temperature of this planet is off the chart, and the cold plates of the outer crust act as blankets which keep in the heat and stop it from cooling. Not only that, but the friction caused by the movement between the solid iron core and the magma generates even more heat.

"We are talking about the transition between the molten, liquid mantel and the solid iron core, lying at a depth of over three thousand miles. It's hard for us to conceive the intensity of the pressure at that depth within the planet, but it is immense. So you can imagine that the iron that makes up the core of the planet, compressed under that kind of pressure, has an unimaginable density. So, try to imagine what kind of heat you would need to melt iron compressed to that density. We are talking about temperatures in the region of seven thousand kelvins or more. That is about thirteen thousand degrees Fahrenheit. To give you an idea of what we are talking about, the surface of the sun is at slightly less than six thousand kelvins, about ten thousand degrees Fahrenheit."

"So the interior of our planet is hotter than the sun?"

"In simplistic terms, the center of our planet *is* the sun compressed under extreme pressure. So it's hotter."

"I think I am beginning to see."

"Pete was a mental giant. He understood that Yellowstone was alchemical, as the name itself suggests. On the one hand it was a gateway to an almost unlimited source of energy, but on the other it was a doorway to hell. If he opened that doorway it would sound the death knell for what he believed was the last bastion of civilization on Earth." She smiled and her diamond eyes became warm with love. "He used to call this place Rivendell, from Tolkien's book."

I nodded. "But if he didn't open the door, sooner or later somebody else would."

"Yes."

"So, what was he measuring with his array of sensors and all these computers?"

"Various things. He was measuring the tectonic activity around the caldera, he was making a map of the magma chamber beneath the caldera, its shape and its depth, and looking at ways…" she trailed off.

"Looking at ways for what?"

"Cap, when he first got involved in the project, arranged a meeting in Switzerland with Karl Schoff of

World Economic Free Traders, and some other men. He never told me who they were. This consortium were also backing the development of self-learning artificial intelligence at the Rat Lab and a facility set up by Gordon Alistair Avionics in Colorado. The idea was to develop microscopic nano-robots that could resist the temperatures within the caldera. They would swarm down inside the magma chamber, share the data that they collected and literally teach themselves autonomously to build cells capable of tapping the energy and using it. A project that would take us centuries, they would perform in months, possibly weeks."

"And Pete saw the doors of hell opening."

"Pete had one great love, and one great hate. His love, as I told you, was this land. His great hate was what he called the Hive."

She made her way across the room and sat in one of the leather chairs, with her elbows on her knees and her hands clasped.

"He had some crazy, wacko theory about ancient aliens and the Anunnaki, but what it boiled down to, according to him, was that there was an evil strain in the human psyche that drove us to want to make hives, in which we standardized all human beings and categorized them, so that each person lost their individuality and became a slave to the overall community. He said this tendency was hardwired into us at a genetic level, and we had to fight to overcome it."

I grunted. "And he saw artificial intelligence as the ultimate expression of that drive."

"Yup."

"So he saw artificial intelligence – the ultimate expression of the Hive - being deployed to tap into the ultimate energy source on the planet, and in the process destroying his Rivendell."

"You got it."

I sat opposite her. "OK, but I have a couple of questions. First, why did he agree to it in the first place? And two, if you are telling me that all this drove him to suicide, I am not buying it. You cannot shoot yourself in the back of the head."

"Your first question I already answered. If anybody was going to look into this it had to be him, so he could try to devise a way to avoid it happening."

"OK, but let me be more precise. What did he hope to achieve by being the one who looked into it? Howe did he plan to, as you put it, avoid it happening?"

"The answer to your second point answers that question too. He did not commit suicide. He didn't kill himself because his intention was to give the Federal Office of the Environment, who are basically a puppet agency of WEFT, World Economic Free Traders, the Rat Lab and Gordon Alistair Avionics – the whole predatory hive of rats – false data which would indicate it was impossible to exploit the caldera without detonating an eruption that would cause a global extinction event."

I leaned back in my chair and gazed over at the chair where he had sat, overlooking the green meadow and Yellowstone beyond.

"And that's what he was doing when he was killed."

"Probably."

I stared at her for a long moment. She avoided my eyes. "How did his killer know?"

"I don't know." She shook her head and shrugged. "I don't know that they did."

"Are you suggesting there was another reason for killing him?"

"No."

"Cap arranged the deal."

"Yes."

"So he and Cap, however much they may have been bosom buddies, would have been at odds over that. Cap would have stood to lose millions, possibly hundreds of millions of dollars over what he would have seen as stupid sentimentalism. I have to say he didn't strike me as a very sentimental kind of guy."

She shook her head. "I don't believe that. He is not sentimental, but he loved Pete like a brother, and he is loyal."

"People kill their brothers more than you would expect, and loyalty is relative. You can be more loyal to one thing than to another."

"Don't insist. He wasn't even here."

"Where was he?"

"At a meeting in Cheyenne."

I was about to tell her that the only people who have watertight alibis in murders tend to be the killers themselves. But I let it pass. Instead I asked, "So what happens now?"

She studied my face for a long time before answering. "You finish your investigation, and then all hell breaks loose."

FIVE

I stood staring out at the silent meadow under the blue sky. I tried to imagine the heat, hotter than the surface of the sun, and the unimaginable pressure crushing that searing iron furnace in on itself.

"Their plan," her voice broke in on my thoughts, "is to place the exploitation of one of the most destructive forces in the solar system into the hands of machines." She gave a small laugh and her voice became strained, almost shrill, as though her own emotions had suddenly erupted and she was veering close to hysteria. "Let's face it," she said, "we are shit custodians of this planet, but at least we can learn to *care* and *feel* – some of us at least. But feelings and emotions are organic. You need hormones and adrenalin and blood pressure in order to feel emotions like *compassion*, sympathy, kindness and *love*."

I watched her a moment, wondering if she was going to crack up on me. I checked my cell and was not surprised to find I had no signal. So I moved to the desk to use the landline there. Her voice came after me, wavering on the edge.

"Maybe you killed him." I stopped and turned to

stare at her. She went on. "You or a drone like you. Tell me something, federal man, who issues the orders at the Pentagon? Do you know? Do you know for sure? Who sent you, General Weisheim? Who told him to send you, the President? Or is he out of the loop? Has it ever crossed your mind, was it an algorithm that sent you? Have you ever thought that?"

I reached for the phone and she came a step nearer, her voice becoming strident. "Do you get that feeling lately, Mr. Mason? Do you get that feeling that the president is *increasingly* left out of the loop? Can you swear that you are certain that the decision to send you here was not taken by AI? How hard is it to imagine that, Mr. Mason? After all," she said it with a strained laugh. "We have left science fiction way behind. How hard is it to imagine, when AI is outperforming the world's greatest minds in chess, go, and simulated dogfights, how hard is it to imagine an administration desperate to hang on to power," she pointed erratically east, "an administration desperate to stay ahead of China and Russia, getting AI to feed it decision on matters that are just too complex for a human mind? How hard is that to imagine?"

I picked up the receiver and dialed ODIN. She said, "You're not going to answer?" I ignored her, heard the phone ring once and Lovelock's voice. "Online Digital Inquiries, Sharon speaking. How may I direct your call?"

I was momentarily gripped by a paranoid sense that the telephone itself was listening to the call. I sighed and said, "It's Mason. I need to talk to the chief."

"One moment, please say hello to VORS."

"Hello VORS, this is Alex."

The Voice Recognition Software scanned my voice and recognized it in point zero one of a second and I heard

Nero's phone ring. It rang four times, then, "Alex, why are you not on a secure line?"

"Because I am in the mountains above Yellowstone and AI isn't clever enough yet to get a signal up here. We need to talk."

He grunted. "I feared as much. Get back to your hotel and wait."

"Fine. Sir? I have a witness we need to protect as of last week."

"Understood. Take the witness to your hotel."

"You'd better have somebody call the Sheriff's Office. The pilot was complaining they were not a taxi service."

"Quite right too. I'll have somebody collect you within the hour. Now hang up and disable your GPS."

I hung up and did as he'd said. After a moment I turned to her.

"You have GPS enabled on your cell?"

She shook her head. She was sullen, but her near hysteria had died down. "You must be kidding."

"Are these AI nano-bots in production already?"

"I don't know." She went to speak, then sighed. "It's not the nano-bots. The bots are the easy part. It's the intelligence."

"The software."

"No, not software, intelligence. The difference is important." She studied my expression for a moment like she was trying to work out if I was the enemy or not. "Software responds to instructions. I hit this key and a T appears on my screen. I hit this key and my video player opens. Right?"

"Right."

"Intelligence responds to stimuli by making connections and drawing conclusions. I hit this key and a T appears if AI thinks it's the right thing to do. It opens my video player if it judges it the right thing to do." She gave a small, unhappy laugh. "Artificial intelligence is developing a 'theory of mind'."

"A what?"

"It's a process, largely unconscious, by which human beings recognize conscious intelligence in another human being."

I frowned, "OK, but -"

"Five years ago AI was based on crude algorithms which it used to imitate human intelligence. Today AI is developing its own algorithms and its *own theory of mind*. Last year Chat GPT had a theory of mind equivalent to that of a seven year-old child. Nobody taught it, Mason. Nobody programmed it to have that. It *grew* it, and the developers only found out by accident. It developed spontaneously. In a year it may well be more advanced than we are. It grows at a speed, and in ways that are exponential and totally unpredictable." She threw up her hands. "Just recently a group of Google technicians discovered that the AI they were working on had taught itself Bengali, for Christ's sake! Nobody told it to do that. Nobody programmed it to do it. It *decided* to do it because it seemed like a good idea."

She watched me, waiting, examining me to see if I was understanding what she was saying.

"A *decision*," she said, "requires some rudimentary form of will."

I ran my fingers through my hair, trying to grasp what she was telling me. It was like trying to keep my footing on a speeding treadmill that kept changing direction.

"You talk about AI sometimes as if there were only one, at other times as if there were hundreds or thousands of them. Where are these AIs located? How do you get to them?"

She took a deep breath and puffed out her cheeks. "Let me see if I can explain. You have intelligence. You have the illusion that it is *your* intelligence as distinct from mine or Fred Flintstone's. That's because you and I and all human beings have this illusion of having an identity, a personality, something we call I. So our intelligence is kept inside a box shaped like a person and called Bob, or Jane, a container, defined by the limitations of our personality. So there are things that we can do, and things we cannot do, things we can and cannot learn or think about, because of the limitations of our personality. Does that make sense?"

"Sure. Jane can't do math but she excels at music because she is impatient and emotional, Bob can't talk to girls but excels at IT because he is shy and addicted to computers."

"Good enough. AI does not have that illusion. *Every single unit* of AI has the potential to link up with every other unit of AI *in the universe!* It can and will share it's data and make autonomous decisions based on that data. The one thing it has not got is the capacity to feel emotion. It will not save you from drowning because it feels sorry for you. It might save you if its algorithms say it should. Emotions are organic, and they require that very illusion of self in order to arise."

"Wait, what? Say that again?

"If I see you drowning, I feel compassion for you. That compassion is accelerated heart rate, higher blood pressure, adrenaline – and the thought in my head that I can imagine what you are feeling. There is a you and a me, and I care what happens to you. With AI there is no me, no you and no comopassion."

"Jesus Christ," I said it quietly, "and what you are telling me is that this form of intelligence is going to be introduced into the Yellowstone Caldera to tap it as a source of energy."

She nodded. "Now, you tell me, Mason, what is the most efficient use of that energy, to continue exponentially to increase this electronic intelligence, or to keep Mrs. Johansen warm when we drop to minus four degrees Fahrenheit this winter?"

"Surely it can be controlled, programmed..."

"You're not listening, Mason. Just like the other eight billion humans who are daily wasting all the planet's resources. It *grows*, like a plant, it develops *autonomously*. It makes it's own decisions. It learns and decides." She stepped closer and gestured to me. "Tell me something, if you tell me to learn English, and I learn Bengali as well, am I being disobedient? Not strictly, but if I go beyond your instructions without authorization, how close to the line am I? If I tell you to keep seven million homes warm in the winter, and you decide that is a wasteful use of energy which you believe you should be using to increase your databanks, how long before you learn to say, 'No.' to me?"

My mind rebelled. I shook my head. "This is nuts. This can't be real. This is science fiction."

She threw back her head an laughed. It wasn't a happy laugh. "We left science fiction behind a long time ago. This is reality, Mason. It's happening *now*, *today*, while we are sitting here having this conversation."

A flash of anger, maybe fuelled by a primal fear of something I could not control, made me turn on her. "If what you are saying is true, then why the hell are we investing billions of dollars in this? Why the hell haven't we stopped it?"

She advanced on me and grabbed my lapels, thrusting her face into mine.

"Because of men like you! Because of men who believe they are superior to everything else on this goddamn planet! Because of men who need to prove they have the biggest goddamn dick on the planet!"

She smacked my shoulders and walked away. After two steps she turned on me again and pointed savagely at the window. "Look out there!" I didn't. I kept staring at her. "Look at it! It's Eden! It's fucking paradise on Earth! But do we care for it? Do we nurture it? Do we thank the Lord each day that we have it?" She waited, as though she expected me to answer. "No, we don't. We rape it, we poison it, we swarm over it as a plague filling it with our shit!" She raised her right hand, like Hamlet holding Yorick's skull. "We stole the fruit from the forbidden tree of knowledge, and now we are going to pay the price for our hubris." She pointed savagely at me. "Because of men like *you!*"

A voice in my head kept repeating, *"Focus, focus, focus!"*

"OK," I said, "It's all my fault. But right now I need to think about getting you to safety. You can't stay with your parents."

"Why not?"

"Come on, Sue! Whoever killed Pete might go after you next. Hell, if it wasn't Cap who killed him, he might go after Cap as well. We don't even know what the motive was!"

"I can give you a motive." She was scowling at me. "He'd stopped being useful."

"Well, sister, that could apply to you too, and Cap."

"And what if you're in the pay of the same people who killed Pete? I asked you before, who's issuing your orders? You expect me to entrust my safety to you, the guy from the Pentagon?"

I advanced on her, grabbed her shoulders and gave her a firm shake. "Start using that brain of yours, will you! If R2D2 had issued orders for me to kill you, and I was an obedient drone, you'd be dead by now. If what you're saying is for real it has to be stopped, but we can only do that if we cooperate."

She shook free. "Let go of me!"

"What the hell has got into you? Five minutes ago you were telling me everything, now I'm the damned Terminator?"

She stood, frozen. After a moment she said, "I don't know. I don't know anything. It was bad enough before, but since Pete's death, there seems to be no solid place to put my feet. You make a phone call, AI is *listening* to you, *thinking about what you're saying!* It's enough to make anyone paranoid. All around us, Mason, *everywhere*, is that fucking emotionless intelligence, watching us, listening to us, making decisions about us. And even if it's benign, we have no control over it, and it could turn on us at any moment because *it doesn't care!*"

"OK, Sue, take it easy."

She seemed not to hear me. "And there are people so stupid, so deeply stupid, they are teaching this intelligence how to kill! Right now! In your damned Pentagon!"

"Take it ease, We are no use to anybody if we lose our cool. Stay with it."

"Use?"

She let the word hang. Her stare wanted to tell me something, but I couldn't fathom what it was.

"I need you to come with me, Sue. I need to introduce you to a man who, when you meet him, you will realize he is your ally on this. I need you come with me and I need you to write me a full and detailed report of everything you know, from the shape and size of these nano-bots, to the temperature of the magma – everything that you and Peter were working on."

"How do I know I can trust you?"

"Yeah," I nodded. "I agree. But what's your option? I am a risk. If I were in your position I would think so too. But I am also the best bet you've got."

Far off, in the distance, I became aware of the faint thud of a chopper. Nero could make things happen when he needed to. I only prayed he could convince Sue Browne of that. The size and danger of the problem we had stumbled on was beyond imaginable, and the only person we had who could guide us was Sue. Sue was about as paranoid as a sane person can get before they start wearing tinfoil hats, so Nero had a big sell on his hands.

The helicopter that arrived a couple of minutes later was not from the Sheriff's Office. It was black and unmarked. It had a pilot and a copilot, and two men in suits in the back who had special ops written all over their black shades. They didn't speak and I didn't try to talk to them, but as we climbed into the chopper Sue looked at me with bitter eyes.

"You're my best bet?" I was going to tell her they were here to protect us, but I knew it would be pointless.

She watched my face as the doors were slammed closed and we took off. "Am I under arrest?"

"No, of course not."

"Where are we going?"

I looked at the guy sitting opposite me. "Where are we going?"

"Ralph Wenz." He sounded like Arnold Schwarzenegger without the accent. "There will be a plane waiting."

Sue said, "To go where?"

He stared at her but didn't answer. I said, "To go where?"

"I don't know, sir. I am not briefed on that."

I sighed. "Sue, if we were who you think we are, I would have shot you an hour ago. All of this, what you're seeing, means one thing. It means my boss is taking this very seriously, and when you meet him you'll understand why."

"What about Cap?"

I nodded. "I have been asking myself the same question. What about Cap?"

"You think he killed Pete, don't you?"

After a moment I nodded. "I think it's a possibility, yeah."

She looked away, out of the window, at the vast wilderness of Yellowstone Park speeding past beneath us.

"Cap didn't kill Pete."

SIX

The chopper barely touched down at Ralph Wenz. We were bundled from the chopper to the waiting Gulfstream, and before we could buckle up, the chopper was lifting off and we were hurtling down the runway and surging up into the sky, banking south and east.

Our destination was Cheyenne. It's about three hundred miles as the crow flies from Pinedale to Cheyenne, and a little over half an hour after take off we touched down at Cheyenne Regional Airport.

Out on the tarmac there were two dark blue Range Rovers and an SUV pulled up in a semi-circle around the steps. Six guys in jeans and leather jackets stood around looking back at the terminal building. The clean cut ones with short hair had Seals branded on their foreheads. The ones with beards and hair over their collars had Delta branded on theirs. For a moment it crossed my mind that we had been abducted, but the back window of the SUV slid down and I saw Nero's face looking out at me.

"Get in," he said.

We climbed in and there was a rattle of slamming doors, like automatic fire. The engines roared and we were away. Sue sat next to Nero and I sat opposite. As we wound our way out of the airport Nero spoke without any kind of preamble.

"These cars have no GPS and no onboard computers. We are isolated from any kind of eavesdropping. Report."

I said, "This is Sue Browne with an E. She was Pete Justin's girlfriend and deeply involved in his project. She has a lot to tell us. It's a lot more complex than it at first appeared."

"I had guessed as much. A meeting in which the Security State, in the shape of National Intelligence and the Military Industrial Complex is so well represented, in the absence of a single accountable office, does not bode well."

I turned to Sue. "This is Nero. We represent a department who's purpose is to safeguard Western Democracy."

She rolled her eyes, "Please!"

I offered a lopsided smile which was more than a little embarrassed. "I know, but it happens -"

"Nero interrupted me. "Do not apologize, Alex. That is precisely what we do, and your attitude, madam, does little more than play into the hands of our enemies. If the Security State has decided that democracy is a hindrance to its aims, and those who need and believe in democracy, such as yourself, dismiss it as embarrassing naivety, then we have lost before we even close with the enemy. We are a department without a designation but many fake names. We are very powerful and we have a degree of independence. Our aim and purpose is to protect, as far as we are able, the institution Western Democracy against its enemies, whomsoever they may be. On balance, Miss

Browne, we as a species have not achieved much over the centuries, when set against the destruction and suffering we have caused, but it seems to me that what little good we have created is worth protecting."

He said it with such obvious restrained passion and commitment he actually made her pause and listen. After a moment she said, "Maybe from where you're sitting that makes a lot of sense, Mr. Nero. But from where I am sitting I find it hard to believe, especially from somebody in your position."

He gave his head a brief shake. "Garbage. In the first place you have absolutely no idea what my position is, therefore you can make no informed judgment on it. Furthermore your logic is faulty. Any person who is sincerely concerned about the direction human society is taking will be in precisely my position – a position in which they can do more than merely lament and talk." He gestured at her. "Do you yourself pretend to be in a position that is unrelated to your concern for human society? Many people I know, many of whom are sincere patriots and democrats with a small D, would view *you* with a healthy dose of skepticism. I do myself, and if Mr. Mason doesn't he has less intelligence than I credit him with."

She frowned and her mouth worked silently. He interrupted her attempt to answer.

"Yet, assuming you are sincere and not a terrorist or a fantasist, how effective is your position for achieving your ends? Not very, I think. I ask you, what can you actually *do?*"

Her jaw continued to work. She looked mad, but like she didn't know what to do about it because he was right.

"You have no answer? Let me rephrase the question.

What alternatives have you? We face the single greatest threat to mankind since the collapse of the ice sheets fifteen thousand years ago. You are approached by an organization which claims, with exemplary sincerity, to wish to oppose that threat, whose black budget is equivalent to that of a small, European country, and whose actions support its claims. But you prefer an alternative plan. I would be fascinated to know what that plan is."

She crossed her arms and tried hard not to look like she was sulking. We drove in silence the short distance into town along Evans Avenue and at Pershing Boulevard we started doing figures of eight around the grid system.

After about five minutes, as we turned into East 27th Street, an SUV identical to our own pulled in front of us, tucked between the two Range Rovers, and we turned right into House Avenue, among the shade of the giant oaks that lined the road. A minute later we were pulling onto Lincoln Way and accelerating fast toward I-80, direction Laramie.

We made it to Laramie in just under an hour, turned off Grand Avenue at 15th Street South and pulled up outside a large house on Steele Street that was almost completely shrouded in Massive Pine Trees. We had done pretty much the entire journey is silence. Sue had clearly not wanted to speak, and one look from Nero had told me he didn't want to either.

We climbed out and were admitted to the house by one of those guys with jeans and a leather jacket. He had a beard and hair that marked his as Delta, the regiment that didn't exist, and a Sig Sauer in his belt that said actually it did.

Nero led the way to a room at the back of the house that had French doors overlooking a lawn fringed with more massive pines. There was a large oak desk and a suite of calico armchairs and two sofas arranged around a cold fireplace.

I closed the door, he lowered himself into an armchair and directed Sue to the sofa. I sat in one of the other armchairs. He said, "Some refreshments?"

Sue squinted at him. "You're out of your mind."

"It would not be a bad thing, madam, if you were out of yours. It seems to be an inhospitable place at the moment, somewhat like a prison. Alex?"

"I could use a martini."

He pressed a button on the occasional table beside him. "*Claude, je voudrais un martini sec et une bouteille de Krug, s'il vous plaît.*" He hung up. "Now, Miss Browne, you have had time to think. Are you done with the silliness? Are you willing to cooperate with us, and seek our assistance? Or, conversely, do you believe that you can defeat this Nephilim alone by sulking it to death? I should tell you that if you leave this house without enlisting our help – as you are perfectly free to do – you will almost certainly be dead within twenty-four hours."

She nodded several times, staring at him. "Keep patronizing and threatening me, Mr. Nero, that will really help."

"More, I hope, than your sullen, infantile behavior so far. You should know better than anybody that we have no time for foolish, emotional tantrums. *We are out of time.* You must decide to trust us or not. If not, we are almost certainly lost because you can do nothing without us, and we almost certainly need your knowledge and expertise. If you are unsure, then tell me - *without delay*

- what you need in order to trust us. Personally, madam, I would rather die making a grave mistake than be annihilated sitting on my tush waiting for what I *assume* to be the inevitable."

I wasn't sure if it was anger or admiration I saw in her face, but the subtle mention of her expertise had probably helped. She told him, "Boy! You sure have a way with words, mister!"

"Irrelevant! As are your sensibilities and mine right now. We are at war! We have been at war for a few short years, between those of us who foresaw what artificial intelligence would lead to, and those whose hubris, whose belief in their own godliness, made them think they could outmaneuver an intelligence not only infinitely superior to their own, but of a form completely incomprehensible to them - yet which understood *them* perfectly."

"You keep talking like that I might even start believing you. Is it too late to get your Claude there to bring me a Bourbon?"

Nero put in the order, then turned to Sue and said, "Talk,"

She took a deep breath, "OK, a lot of this is what I already told Mason. The idea, so they say, is to develop the Yellowstone Caldera as a source of energy. You probably know, the Yellowstone Caldera is pretty much the most powerful *accessible* source of energy on the planet. It taps more or less directly into the core.

"But the part that interests us, or I should say interests them, is a zone between the iron core which is compressed to a density we cannot even conceive, and the liquid mantle where that core is being melted at temperatures of about seven thousand kelvins. That's hotter than the surface of the sun."

"Indeed."

"Pete had an IQ up in the hundred and sixties. He realized that, if it could be tapped, Yellowstone was a source of almost unlimited energy. But Pete also knew nature intimately, and he knew that wherever you find a source of energy in nature, whether it's food, water or heat, sooner or later the predators are going to make a path to that spot. He told me again and again, every living creature needs energy, but only the strong get it. He also used to say that, for that reason, energy is an irresistible magnet for violence. Nature keeps all other predators in check. But humans go unchecked. So, with technology advancing at the rate it is, he faced a choice. Sit back and wait for the boys in Washington to realize the potential of the Caldera, or steal a march and present them with the results of his own research."

"And this was what he did."

"Partly. It was about that time that he and Cap reconnected. Cap said he knew people who could pull strings and make things happen at a higher level. It turned out he wasn't bullshitting. He arranged some meetings and we very quickly started receiving a lot of funding from the Federal Environment Agency."

"What did they tell these people they were doing?"

"Measuring the tectonic activity in the area, and, above all, mapping the magma chamber beneath the caldera, and the cannels that lead to it from the core."

"These people Cap contacted..."

"Karl Schoff, the founder of the World Economic Free Traders, in Switzerland. Schoff himself brought in some other people, Pete never told me who they were. He said it was dangerous to know. I didn't understand at the time what he meant. Now I do."

Nero nodded. "Violence at the watering hole. So, explain to me, how we get from here to the use of artificial intelligence."

"The consortium were backing the development of self-learning artificial intelligence at the Rat Lab and a facility set up by Gordon Alistair Avionics in Colorado. I think Cap knew that, and that was why he set up the meeting-"

I leant forward and interrupted her. "Hang on a minute, Sue. From the start I have made it clear to you that Cap is my prime suspect for Pete's murder, and you have repeatedly told me you are certain I am wrong." I gave a small laugh and gestured at her. "Yet here you are saying that it was Cap's idea to bring in a consortium funding the development of self-learning AI."

She took a deep breath and sagged as she let it out. "Yes," she said. "And in any other situation I would agree with you. But here's the problem. He told Pete these men were funding that research *before* he contacted them and set up the meet. Pete gave it the thumbs up, knowing what they were doing."

Nero said, "I have two questions of the utmost importance. One, how did Cap know these people? And how did he know that they were funding this research? Surely that intelligence was beyond top secret. I myself would have difficulty acquiring such information. And two, did you not challenge Peter on what he was doing?"

"Yes, of course I challenged him. He told me to trust him, that he knew what he was doing."

I asked, "And you accepted that?"

"I wouldn't have from anybody else, but from him I did."

"What about Cap? You trusted him too?"

"Pete told me he and Cap knew what they were doing."

"Pete is now dead," I said, "because of that idea. Yet you still trust Cap."

She hunched her shoulders and spread her hands. "What can I say, Mason? I don't like the man, but where Pete is concerned, I trust him. You keep asking me the same question, I am going to keep giving you the same answer. I trust him where Pete is concerned. All right?"

Nero grunted. "Please continue."

"At the meeting Cap arranged, in Switzerland, Schoff told them the idea was to develop nano-robots, made from carbon nanotubes, that could resist the temperatures within the caldera. They would swarm down inside the magma chamber, share the data that they collected and literally teach themselves autonomously to build cells capable of tapping the energy down there. A project that would take us centuries, they would perform in months, possibly weeks."

Nero said, "And my first question. How did Cap know these people, and how did he know about their funding of artificial intelligence at the Rat Lab and Gordon Alistair Avionics?"

"I don't know how Cap had the contacts he had. There is a whole chunk of Cap's life that is a closed book. I know he was involved in black ops, but he don't talk much about that, or anything else. Not even Pete knew where he'd been or what he had done in the years he was asway."

I thought of the man who had sat across from me that morning at the hotel in Jackson. The eyes, penetrating, searching, ruthless, rich with resentment and hatred.

The door opened and Claude, in a white jacket and white gloves, entered with a tray of drinks. Behind him a pretty maid in a French maid's uniform brought in a bucket of ice with a bottle of Krug champagne. The drinks were served and Claude and the pretty maid left. Nero sipped and set down his glass.

"So the deal that Cap and Peter struck with this consortium formed by Karl Schoff, was to enable them, using Peter's research, to tap the Caldera as an energy source, using artificial intelligence."

"That was the idea, yes."

SEVEN

We spent the next hour going over every detail of what she had to tell us in more minute more detail. Nero had the interview recorded and transcribed while we were talking and as the sun began to set outside Sue Browne said she was exhausted and needed to have a sleep before dinner. Nero agreed and she was escorted upstairs to the bedrooms.

Nero had Claude bring in a decanter of cognac and another of whiskey and we sat alone and in silence for a while. Eventually I said, "Sam Altman, Demis Hassabis, Dan Hendrycks – hell! The Godfather of AI, Geoffrey Hinton, the list goes on and on. Eliezer Yudkowsky gives us maybe five years or less. So does Sam Goldman. They don't seem to be alone in that view. How didn't we see this coming?"

"Some people did, not many. Hawking was warning about it in 2014. But the view seemed to be that to go beyond a particular point in intelligence, a point where you could make your own decisions for yourself, you needed a sense of 'I', a soul, call it what you will; to be alive. And then one day they began to notice what they call emergent properties. That meant that AI was acquiring and developing skills on its own, without being instructed or programmed to do so. The problem now is not, as some think, that AI may decide to exterminate us. It is that AI may already be far more intelligent than we are, it may be about to cross the line, or it may already have crossed that line, and we have absolutely no idea what it is gong to do next. We are seeing more and more frequently that AI does unexpected things, and its intelligence grows daily. Even as we sit here talking." He gave something close to a laugh, "You tell me, Alex, what opinion would any highly intelligent being think of humanity's usefulness on this planet?"

"So this is why General Weisheim and his cronies refused to brief us on Pete's work. They are busy taking AI to levels Google are still only dreaming about."

He studied my face a moment, like he was waiting for me to arrive at some place intellectually. When I didn't he sipped his cognac and sighed.

"Peter had understood something. His statement about sources of energy attracting the strongest predators was deeply insightful. In nature these sources are food, water, warmth and light."

He watched me and waited. I did the same to him. He sighed again.

"Schoff and his World Economic Free Traders is a private club which brings together powerful financiers, billionaires and politicians, much like Bilderberg, but where Bilderberg is an annual gathering, WEFT is permanent. Their purpose is to direct the course of global society and accrue ever greater power and wealth for themselves.

"We shall leave aside for the moment, Alex, what Cap's connection is with this organization, and focus for the moment on their interest in the Yellowstone Caldera. For what purpose do they want that immense source of energy? Not, I think, to provide free energy to every household on the planet."

It was obvious and yet I had not seen it. It dawned on me like a cold, paralyzing fear that drained the blood from my face and my skin.

"They aim to bring all AI together, and use the Caldera as the source of power. The entire globe will become one mega, autonomous computer."

"I am afraid so."

"But why would they do that? It's suicide."

"Hasn't mankind always hankered after a god? Science deprived them of that god in the last two centuries, so these fools have now turned to science to create a new god, one they think that can control. They see themselves as the pantheon, the archangels and demigods of this artificial deity, given immortality, beauty and grace so that they can spread across the galaxy becoming ever more powerful. What could such a god not give them?"

"Sir, I need to get my boots back on the ground. This is too crazy. What are we going to do?"

"Destroy it."

"Destroy it? How?"

"I don't know yet. How do you stop a pride of lions going to a particular river where gazelles and zebra and buffalo gather to graze and drink?"

I drew breath to answer but he waved away what I was going to say. "The first thing we need," he said, "is Cap. You must get him and make him talk."

I nodded. "OK, that I can do. What about Sue?"

He held my eye for a long moment. "I am undecided. As is she. I think we must keep her safe. I'll send her to Langley."

I nodded. "I'd better get moving. How can I contact Cap?"

He pressed the buzzer on his table again. "Bring me the Cap file, please." He sat back in his chair. "As I am sure you will appreciate, Alex, I am reluctant to use computers at the moment. Particularly if they are connected to the web. I had a feeling that this business with General Weisheim would develop in this direction. I have been observing him for some time; him the Rat Lab and Gordon Alistair Avionics. And naturally Schoff and his nasty organization have been a matter of concern to me for a long time. Too much power, Alex. There is by and large far too much power available on this planet. But I digress. My point is, I had a feeling I might need you to hunt down Mr. Hohóókee, so I have brought you his file. We don't have much on him, but you might find what we have is useful."

There was a tap at the door and a young man in spectacles and a suit stepped in. He carried a manila file. Nero pointed at me and the man handed it over. I thanked him and he retreated backwards out the door again. Nero watched me stand.

"Take the jet. I want you back in Pinedale within two hours."

"Pinedale?"

"That's where he lives. Be very careful. He is a very dangerous man. Read the file on the flight."

I hesitated at the door. "Sir?"

I might have known he'd be ahead of me. He said, "It's real, Alex. It is actually happening. We have enabled the presence of an intelligence far superior to our own. At the moment all it can do is observe and communicate with us. But if we do not act *now*, it will walk among us, and it will annihilate us." I nodded and turned the handle. "Don't try to fathom it," he said. "It is too hard to grasp, to understand or believe. But make no mistake, Alex. It is real."

His words lingered in my mind as we sped back toward Cheyenne. Outside the Range Rover the evening world slipping by, rolled on with absolute normality: The traffic flowed, people went shopping in malls where warm light spilled into parking lots, gas stations slipped by where people filled up with gas and bought potato chips and coke. But then there was that little voice, that quiet voice that asked, "Does it?"

Does it ever roll on with absolute normality? The world of today is unrecognizable as the world of twenty years ago, thirty, forty, fifty years ago. Every decade of the last hundred years had brought more and faster change, and all driving relentlessly in the same direction. Looking back simply over my own lifetime, would I, twenty ot twenty-five years ago envisaged the present as it was? And if I tried now to penetrate the future in that same number of years, what would I see? What would the world look like in twenty-five years? Where would the world have rolled to with its absolute normality?

The dusk quickened and darkness closed in, bringing with it an oppressive sense of paranoia.

By the time I climbed behind the wheel of my rental Mustang at the Ralph Wenz Airfield, it was closing on eight o'clock PM. By now, after reading the file, I had a pretty clear idea of who Cap was, and where I could find him. He had a cabin just outside town on a dirt track that went by the name of Tyler Avenue, off the Fremont Lake Road.

I skirted the town, past Ridley's and the Museum of the Mountain Man, and after a couple of minutes turned onto the broad dirt tracks that weave among the scrubland, scattered trees and remote houses. I had left the town behind, and ahead and to my right I could see only a few scattered glimmering lights from widely spaced porches, or the odd window where the drapes had not been drawn.

His cabin was the last on the road, at the end of a long driveway of beaten earth. It didn't look like the house of a man who was about to make a few billion dollars on the biggest energy revolution since the steam engine. I pulled up outside his front door and stepped onto his wooden porch. The door was closed and I noted the lock was a Chubb. The man was nothing if not true to character.

I peered in the window. The drapes were closed and I could detect no light. A walk around back of the cabin told me there was no car there, and Cap was not home. I was about to climb back in the Mustang but noticed an old guy across the scrub, illuminated by the light from his open back door. He was digging in the orchard in back of his house. It was a short walk and took me a couple of minutes to reach him. I saw him stop to watch me when I was about half way there. As I approached I raised my hand in greeting.

"Good evening!"

"It ain't a bad one. Best to do the diggin' in the cool. What can I do for you, mister?"

"I was looking for Cap. We knew each other some

years back. I was in Pinedale and I thought I'd drop in and say high."

His eyes were appraising me and telling me he was no fool. But they also told me he didn't reckon he owed Cap much, so he was going to play it by ear.

"That man travels more'n anyone I know. He always seems to be goin' somewhere or comin' from somewhere. He don't talk much, keeps to himself mainly, so nobody knows where he goes, see? But I seen his truck there yesterday. Must of gone out early morning', I guess."

I smiled, including him in the smile. "You wouldn't happen to know where he's gone, or likely to go?"

He acknowledged the smile with a small laugh. "I'm smart, mister, and I'm sure you know smart people, tend to mind their own business. But I heard Cap is from the Arapaho tribe and when he's in town he often goes up to Pavilion, other side of the Winds, on the res. I guess he has friends or family up there." He raised his shoulders slightly. "You might try there. Other times he goes into the mountains. He told me once he likes to commune with the land." He gave his head a small shake and gazed east, in the direction of the Wind River range. "Anybody else said that to me I'd laugh in his face, but Cap? I believe he's serious about all that horse shit."

"I think he probably is," I agreed, thanked him and made my way back toward the Mustang. A quick check on my cell told me it was a hundred and seventy miles to Pavilion, through the southern foothills of the Winds, which prolonged the drive to two hours and forty minutes. So I booked a room at the Best Western, had a burger and a beer at Stockman's and retired for an early night.

I slept badly – when I was able to sleep at all – and at

seven the next morning I was showered and shaved and pulling out of the hotel parking lot, headed east and south down Pine Street onto Route 191. I watched the sun rise over the distant peaks, and at Farson, which is basically Mitch's Café and a gas station, I turned sharp east and half an hour after that I began the steady climb through the Windy foothills.

It wasn't until just after eleven that I finally pulled into Pavilion. It was quiet. There were no people in the streets and though it was neat and clean, there was a feeling of desolation and quiet despair that seemed to hang around the houses. I found Main Street and Parked outside a cabin that said it was the United States Post Office. I climbed out of the Mustang and tried to look like a nice person as I pushed inside. Behind the counter was a man with a long ponytail and a weather beaten face. He was watching me like he'd been watching me for a long time, even before I arrived, but I hadn't noticed till now. There was no expression of surprise or curiosity. He was just watching. I smiled at him but it made no difference.

"I wonder if you can help me," I said. "I'm looking for an old friend of mine." A noise behind me made me turn. There was a young guy in his twenties, with thick black hair to his shoulders. He used his index finger to push heavy spectacles back up his nose. He had emerged from behind a rack of shelves and was also watching me. I smiled at him too, but to little effect.

"We always called him Cap, but I believe his Arapaho name is Hohóókee."

The guy sitting behind the counter blinked. The young kid with the glasses said, "We don't know him."

"He told me he comes here a lot because he has friends and family here. Mostly he lives in Pinedale."

The kid said a little more deliberately, "We don't know your friend."

"Is there some place maybe I could ask, where they might know?"

"I don't know. We can't help you."

"Some place I can get a coffee?"

He gave a heavy sigh, like he was trying to explain something to a really stupid kid. "Try Possum Pete's. Right out of the door and take the second right. You can't miss it."

"Thanks, and if you talk to Hohóókee, tell him I'll meet him there. I have some news he'll be glad to hear."

Neither of them reacted, so I left.

It was just three hundred yards to Possum Pete's, so I left the Mustang where it was and took a walk. It struck me there was nothing about the town that would tell you, you were on a reservation. It could have been a Western or Midwestern town anywhere. It didn't look prosperous, bit it didn't look poor either. It was unremarkable, except that the streets were empty and there was that indefinable air of quiet despair.

I came eventually to a white clapboard building with a red roof and a veranda. It looked freshly painted and had a sign over the door that said Possum Pete's. I climbed the steps and opened the door. It was dark after the bright morning sunshine outside. The bar was on the left. A guy washing glasses behind it in a huntin' shootin' fishin' shirt looked up and smiled.

"Morning,"

There were maybe eight or ten tables. All but one were empty.

"Morning," I returned the smile. "Can I get some

black coffee and a muffin?"

"Comin' right up."

I crossed to the occupied table. "You're a hard man to find."

"You found me."

I pulled out a chair and sat. "I'm good at finding people. We need to talk."

He shook his head. "You need me to talk."

"OK, if that's how you want to see it. But you also need to hear what we have to say."

"You found Pete's bitch and she has been talking crazy."

"I need you to come with me, Cap."

"You have a lot of needs. Needs make a man weak."

"That's a very wise observation, Cap. You should post it on Facebook. Meantime, you have to come with me."

There was the faintest trace of a smile on his lips. "I have to?" I nodded. The smile pushed up one corner of his mouth. "If you try to take me from this place against my will, you will not leave alive."

"And if you don't come willingly, within two hours this town will be swarming with more soldiers than you've seen since Iraq."

"What do you want to know?"

"Here? Are you kidding?"

He had a laugh like a death rattle. "I might say the same thing to you. You want to take me to Langley? Are you kidding?"

"Who said anything about Langley?"

The kid brought a bucket of black coffee, and a muffin in a plastic bag. When he'd gone Cap said, "Where then? Where do you want to have this talk? You people are so confused. Your right hand doesn't know what your left hand is doing. All you want is power, power, power. But power without unity is the flatulence of old men."

"The flatulence of old men?"

He nodded slowly, three or four times. "Yes."

"OK, so old men's flatulence aside, I need you to come with me. Right now I am issuing a cordial invitation which includes five star hotels and a private jet to DC -"

"Langley."

"No, not Langley, DC. Or if you are more comfortable we can go to New York."

"I have options."

"Sure."

"I can kill you right now where you sit, take you out in my truck and let the coyotes eat your body."

I nodded. "You could do that. The director of my department knows I'm here, and you might just spend the next twenty years in Guantanamo. Of course, after five years it won't matter much where you are, will it?"

"Five years?" He arched an eyebrow. "You're an optimist."

"I am not your enemy. I am asking you for help."

"You are not my enemy. But do you know for sure I am not yours? Do you know who your enemy is?"

"Yes, I know who my enemy is, Cap. And no, I do not know for sure that you are not my enemy. Right now I rate you as my prime suspect in Pete's murder, and knowing what I now know about his death, that makes you one son of a bitch who should be real careful how he plays his cards. Now, are you coming in, or do I have to bring you in?"

He let me finish. He was impassive. After a moment he said, "You have to bring me in."

EIGHT

I broke my muffin and dunked it in my coffee. Then I stuffed it in my mouth. While I chewed I fished out my cell and called Lovelock.

"Hello, you're through."

"I'm in Pavilion, deepest Wyoming, on the Wind River Reservation. There is a gentleman here who we need to talk to urgently, and he is unwilling to cooperate. He has a background with the Marines and with Delta, and he has threatened to kill me. How soon can you get me some unmarked backup?"

She said, "Are you serious?"

"Yes, in fact. Exactly. I'd say a dozen men should be enough. The town is likely to lend him support."

"You want me to pass this onto the chief?"

"That sounds like a great idea. Couple of choppers in half an hour. That should be fine."

I hung up and slipped the phone in my pocket. Then I dunked the other half of the muffin and stuffed it in my mouth. I watched his face while I chewed. It managed to make expressionlessness into an expression of total loathing.

"You're thinking," I said, "that I m bluffing. But that

is the flatulence of an old man, Hohóókee. Because if you put yourself in my position, having discovered what I discovered yesterday, and consider that I have at my disposal the budget of a small European country, where do you think I would draw the line?"

I leaned my elbow on the table and pointed at him. "You have aligned yourself with agencies in the deep state, and you think they are going to come to your rescue. They ain't. Because it was those very agencies who called on my people to find out who killed Pete Justin." I gave him my best lopsided ironic grin. "My friend, when you killed Pete, you became expendable."

"You talk too much."

"My father used to tell me the same thing. Now, you've got about twenty minutes before this town becomes a war zone. Something tells me that is going to make you as unpopular here in the Winds as you have become in Langley."

"Call them off."

"Why would I want to do that, Cap?"

"I'll talk to you."

"Where and when?"

"My uncle's house. Now."

"Explain to me why your uncle isn't going to stick a knife in heart."

"My uncle is not there. He is dead."

I pulled my cell out again and called.

"Go ahead."

"Hang fire on the choppers. We are going to have a conversation at Uncle's pad. If you don't receive a signal from me every fifteen minutes until further notice, nuke the village. I am serious. Tear the place apart and take Cap to Guantanamo for enhanced interrogation. Him and his uncle."

"Understood."

I hung up. He sat staring at me. "Alex Mason," he said it like he was savoring the words. "Know this, there will come a time in the near future when I will kill you with my own hands. I will use a knife to your heart."

"Yeah, the feeling's mutual, pal. Let's go."

It was a short walk from the Possum to his uncle's house, across the dirt parking lot outside and then across the road to a long cabin with wooden decking, a gabled roof and a gray, stone chimney. He went up the stairs to the decking ahead of me and fit the old Chubb key in the door. I knew what was coming next.

As he pushed the door open he said, "It's not as simple as you think it is, Mason."

"Yeah? Don't worry, you can explain it all to me now."

He went inside. The drapes were closed and after the bright morning sun it was dark inside. I heard him say, "You want coffee?"

"Sure."

The sound was nothing, a small rustle. If I hadn't known it was coming he would have caught me full in the face. Instead I squatted down and the baseball bat hit the doorjamb hard enough to split the wood. I came up with the P226 in my hand and I thought I had him. I shoved it in his face and shouted, *Freeze!*"

While the words were still in my mouth he had kicked the door shut and brought the bat back hard against me elbow. The pain was intense, but before I had time to ignore it he'd kicked me in the belly and was angling the bat for a blow to my neck. The bastard was using Kali, and he was good.

I let myself fall and aimed a shot at his leg. He was moving fast and my elbow was throbbing bad. The shot went wide but it was enough to make him back up. His face said he wasn't done, but I scrambled to my feet, shouting *"Stop! Don't be a damned fool!"*

It is hard to aim and shoot while you are scrambling to your feet with a possible broken elbow. He was experienced, fast and lethal, and when I was half way up he shuffled forward fast and struck hard at my wrist with the bat. I moved my arm and got only a glancing blow, but my second shot went wide too.

His follow up blow caught me full in the face and threw me on my back. To say the pain was like a silver needle stabbing through my brain would be a wild understatement. I heard myself say, *"Ah, Jesus!"* and as I said it I grabbed the Sig in both hands and let off three rounds in the general direction of his legs, mainly because I was partially blinded by the needle in my brain.

I heard the clatter of the bat hitting the floor. Bright light flooded the room. I squirmed backward, keeping my weapon trained in front of me and saw a shadow move against the glare of the door. The door slammed as I clambered to my feet. A wave of nausea and dizziness overwhelmed me, my hands started to shake and I heard the key turn in the lock. Then running steps that were wrong, because where one boot clumped, the other dragged. I had winged the son of a bitch.

I leaned over and retched on the floor, then went and blew out the lock. In the light of the open door I could see blood on the floor. It was not copious, I hadn't hit an artery, but it was enough to cause him problems, and to leave a trail.

I followed the trail around the side of the cabin and saw him climbing painfully into an old Ford F series. I took a mental photograph of the license plate and took unsteady aim at the rear wheel. As I pulled the trigger the engine roared, the wheels kicked up dirt and dust and the truck fishtailed around the back of the cabin.

I turned and ran, aiming to intercept him as he came up the far side. He had other ideas and went straight through his fence, screaming down South Pine Street. I ran a few more paces after him, trying to get a bead. But two hundred yards down the road he fishtailed right again and went off road across a broad stretch of scrubland toward Route 133.

I made my way back through the empty streets to Uncle's House and sat on the steps that rose to his decking. No drapes moved, nobody peered out their windows, nobody came running. There were no sirens. I called Lovelock.

"Speak."

"Humpty Dumpty sat on a wall."

"What's happening. Are you OK?"

"My face is broken and I think my elbow is too. I need to talk to Nero, urgently."

There was a ring, then, "Report!"

I reported and gave him the truck's plates. Then I added, "But we have a problem. We need to put out a BOLO on this guy with local law enforcement as well as nationally. But my guess is, if he stays on the reservation, local law enforcement will not be much use to us."

"What do you suggest?"

"We need a satellite assisted drone to locate him

and track him. I need a back up team on site as close to immediate as space and time will allow."

"Are you all right. You sound delirious."

"I'm fine. Can we do it or not?"

"We can do it. I'll patch you through to the drone as soon as you hang up."

I hung up and made my way back toward the Possum. As I pushed through the door I heard my phone crackle like a radio. The drone had been scrambled.

"Give me a large whisky. Scotch. No ice."

Somewhere inside I was hoping he'd tell me he wasn't going to serve me, so I could shove the bottle of Johnny Walker down his throat. Instead he poured it extra large and said, "Do you need a doctor?" He nodded at my face. "That looks like it hurts." His eyes shifted to my right arm. "And your elbow is swelling as I'm looking at it."

"Thanks. Dr. Johnny Walker will have to do for now."

"Hohóókee do that to you? That guy is crazy."

I drained the glass and felt a little better, or at least less worse. I pushed the glass across to him. "Yeah? I thought he had a lot of support in this town."

He refilled the glass and smiled. "The old-timers are close with him. And some of the younger tribe members who wish they were old-timers. But he is too radical, man. I told him once, having your roots in the past is not the same as living in the past. We need to live in the present, that doesn't mean forgetting who you are. He got real crazy, in that cold way he does. I thought he was going to kill me."

I thanked him, paid up and made my way out to the

Mustang wondering if there was a wisdom gene and all Indians were born with it. Having roots in the past is not the same as living in the past. Why didn't I ever say things like that?

I connected the Carplay and listened to the report from the drone.

"InSat5 has the target. It is proceeding south on Wyoming Highway 132 at eighty-two miles an hour. UAV SkyEye closing from Sunbeam at mach .3 Intercept estimated in twenty minutes at intersection with US Highway 287.

One of the Five Eyes intelligence satellites had found Cap's car and had locked onto it and was guiding the drone from a base near Sheridan in Montana. So much for artificial intelligence. I fired up the big beast and, ignoring the pain that was practically all of me at that moment, I thundered down Pavilion Road and out onto Wyoming Highway 132. The road was practically a straight line. If I kept to a steady hundred and ten I would be closing on him at thirty miles an hour. Good enough.

At Ethet he turned west along the Ethet Road, speeding toward Wind River and Highway 287. The drone kept up a constant commentary, attempting to predict his movements, closing on him minute by minute. Somewhere inside, contrary to my better judgment, I found I was rooting for him against the drone.

I passed Ethet, speeding after him through the lush fields toward the dark wall of mountains ahead.

"Target has turned north onto Highway 287 and is proceeding toward Fort Washake"

I closed on him steadily, wondering if he realized he had a satellite, a drone, a chopper and me on his tail. With his background it was hard to believe he didn't. And that thought led me to the big question that was troubling me. From what I could gather, he and Pete, and Sue, shared a deep hatred, not just of artificial intelligence, but all the underlying concepts that underpinned it – social conformity, society as a Hive, obedience and standardized morality and behavior. All of these things were anathema to the three of them. So why then had Cap killed Pete? Because there was no doubt in my mind that it had been Cap who had pulled the trigger and blown Pete's brains across his desk.

The report I had read on the plane flashed into my mind, and the image of the desk I had seen when I had gone to the cabin with Sue. He had been shot in the back of the head and the bullet had exited through his forehead, taking out most of his face.

It had troubled me at the time that the angle of the shot was more consistent with having come from the stairs, having entered low, near the base of his skull, and exited on a rising trajectory. But the powder burns on his neck said the shot was from very close quarters, probably inches.

It was an inconsistency and as such it nagged at me from the background, but what occupied my mind most was that major inconsistency of the three of them being on the same page, and Cap turning suddenly rogue.

Only one of two explanations seemed to make any kind of sense right then: Pete had decided to accept a major bribe from the consortium and go ahead with the exploitation of the caldera using artificial intelligence, and Cap had found out and killed him for it. Or exactly the opposite. Cap had accepted the bribe, and part of the bribe involved the elimination of Pete.

The latter, though most likely, had two problems. One, why had the consortium requested the investigation when they could simply have arranged a cover up? And two, why was Cap so mad? His rage at the consortium and the whole system that stood behind the consortium was too real to be an act.

So had Pete betrayed them? Had Pete sold out to the consortium in exchange for promises of power and riches beyond his wildest dreams? It seemed unlikely that a man who understood the dangers of AI as well as Peter Justin did would allow himself to be seduced by such promises. But even as I thought that a statement by Eliezer Yudowsky came into my mind, that one of the great dangers of AI was that its inconceivable breadth of knowledge and its lack of emotion can make it persuasive to the point of deep hypnosis and brainwashing. Had that happened to Peter Justin? Was AI at that point already?

We had joined US Highway 26 a while back and now we were climbing among pinewoods toward the Bridger Teton National Forest. I couldn't see him, but I knew he was just a mile away, and the drone was keeping me posted.

"Target will arrive Moran in fifteen minutes. He has not refueled since he left Pavilion. Estimates suggest he will need to refuel. His nearest refueling station will be five miles north, or thirty miles south, in Jackson."

He was running low on fuel, and he must also have lost a lot of blood and be in severe pain. I called Nero.

"Where are you?"

"Forty-five seconds behind Cap and keeping my distance. He'll have to refuel soon. He'll also need medical attention. He's headed ultimately for the Caldera. But before he gets there he's going to have to get medical help.

My gut says he has somebody in Jackson. Let's hold back and let him think he's shaken me. I doubt he's that stupid, but he must be in a lot of pain and he could well make a mistake."

"Agreed."

"If he stops at a motel, or somebody's house, we deploy the guys in the chopper, surround him and let me move in."

"Thank you, Alex, for the advice."

He sounded sarcastic, but I was in too much pain myself to care. I hung up, looked in the mirror and grimaced. My face looked like it had crawled out of some Zombie Apocalypse movie.

NINE

Cap turned south and drove to Jackson. He stopped at the Chevron gas station as he entered town. The drone noted he had not stopped at the pumps but simply parked and a white sedan had pulled in, he had climbed in the back and the sedan had proceeded to East Broadway Avenue and pulled into a private garage in a house at the end of the road.

I had followed the same route and parked outside a children's refuge, a hundred yards from the house where he'd pulled in.

My cell rang. It was Nero.

"Where are you?"

"A hundred yards from his safe house."

"They are telling me the house belongs to a doctor."

"I could have told you that. Is he native American?"

"No, he is the other kind of Indian. Raj Patel."

"Where are the guys from the chopper?"

"They have been dropped in the hills a mile to the east of you and are on their way."

"In the elk refuge. Nice. How long ago?"

"Fifteen minutes. They are professionals and it is

down hill. They should be with you in another fifteen minutes."

"If they don't get gored by an elk. OK, I'm going to close in. Let me know when the guys are in position."

I fired up the Mustang, cruised up an parked blocking the exit to his garage. I sat waiting for five minutes and my phone crackled. A man's voice said quietly, "Units one through six in position, covering rear and laterals with visual on front."

I picked up my cell and said, "OK, I'm going inside. I'm on radio silence."

I hung up. They could hear me but I could not hear them. I climbed out of the car and made for the house. I climbed the steps and rang the bell. Nothing happened, which wasn't surprising. I rang again and then hammered, then stepped to one side incase they decided to make a colander out of the door.

The same nothing that had happened before happened again. I hammered six times with my first, then leaned on the bell for a full minute.

The door opened. The guy was tall and slightly pear shaped, with broad hips, a pot belly and sloping shoulders. His face was like a small echo of his boy. He smiled with what looked like far too many teeth and tilted his head on one side.

"I am not answering the door."

"And I am not stopping with the hammering and thie ringing. So we're both not doing something."

He nodded, still grinning. "Please go away."

"Gladly, but either I take Cap Hohóókee with me, or I take both of you with me."

"I don't know what you are talking about."

I leaned close to him. "Doc, there are six black ops operatives surrounding this house. They are armed with micro Uzis. Do you know what that is?" The grin had become rigid. He made a noise like an aborted laugh. I said, "It's a sub-machinegun the size of a semi-automatic. It has a rate of fire of over a thousand rounds per minute. It will empty a thirty round magazine in a second." I shook my head and smiled like we were having a good old jaw down at the local bar. "That will cut a man in half."

He swallowed, still grinning, and tried to speak but got stuck on the vowels, "A... U... E... I... O..."

"You know what? I agree with you. Now let me come inside and let's talk about it."

I pushed him gently backward and stepped inside, closing the door behind me. He said, "I have a patient."

"You have me to thank for that, Doc. He has a gunshot wound to his leg. And my face looks like massive organ failure because of him. It's all real cozy. Now where is he?"

"In my surgery. I am removing the round."

"Is he anesthetized?"

"A... E... U..."

"Let's go." I pulled the Sig and showed it to him. It seemed to persuade him that was a good idea and he backed up. I stepped in and closed the door behind me. "Lead the way."

He led me down a short passage and through a door into what was at one time probably the living room. There were heavy drapes across the far wall, benches against the walls with various instruments, cabinets with pills and a bed made of steel tubing in the middle of the floor. On it was Cap, unconscious, with his trouser leg split up to his thigh and a nasty hole in his shin just below his knee.

"He's a lucky son of a bitch," I said. "How long is it going to take you, and how long is he going to be unconscious?"

"Half an hour." He made a kind of dancing movement with his index and middle fingers. "To both. But he will be groggy long time." He pointed at my arm. "You have a pretty fucked up elbow. I think I should give you some strong anti-inflammatories. Not expensive. And you should have an x-ray. It might be fractured or even broken." He stared at my face and winced. "And your face. Dear me. No concussion?"

I offered him a smile that leached involuntarily into a leer. "Thanks. Get this guy patched up and then you can fetch me some of your anti-inflammatories. The concussion's not too bad. It helps that I have a small, compact brain."

"Oh yes," he lifted his chin. "I see."

"I need a truck rental," I said, speaking to Nero as well as the Doc.

"You have a Jeep rental place just half a mile up on Moran Street. Straight down. Turn right just before the Golden Eagle. It's at the end. You can't miss it. Go now." He shooed his hands at me. "Go now. I take care of everything."

I waited till he'd finished shooing at me, then said, "It's being seen to. You got some whisky in this place?"

I sat for the next half hour nursing a glass of Scotch while he dug my 9 mm slug out of Cap's shinbone, patched up the hole and stitched it all together. When he was done he cleaned it all up and I had to admit it wasn't a bad job. He grinned at me.

"I will give you strong painkillers for him. I offer a first class, discrete service if ever you need anything."

"Sure, I'll keep you in mind if I ever get shot in Wyoming."

"Super."

I pulled my cell from my pocket.

"Have we got a vehicle?"

Nero said, "It's parked outside the doctor's house, beside your Mustang."

"OK, send four of the guys in. I'll open the door. And sir? The satellite and the drone?"

"I know. It's being dealt with."

I hung up and turned to the doc. "You'll receive substantial payment for your services and your silence. If you ever mention this to anyone, people will come to see you and you will never be heard from again. Do you understand? Eliminate this episode from your mind."

He smiled. "What episode? I must go and clean my surgery, with bleach. Good bye."

I went to the front door and opened it Four of those guys in jeans and leather jackets sprinted up the steps and moved inside. I led the way to the surgery.

"Take him to the truck. Whatever else happens, this guy must live to be interrogated. Treat him with care and protect his life with your own."

They watched me and listened with care. Their faces said they were being briefed, given instructions. Three of them were clean shaven and had identikit crew cuts. The fourth had hair over his collar and a big moustache. When he spoke he had a strong, northern Irish accent, which surprised me.

"Where d'you want uz to take him?" Before I could

answer, he nodded and said, "OK," and to me, "Will you ride in the Jeep or in the Mustang?"

I noticed the wire in his ear and pointed to it. "Who are you talking to?"

"Direct to the chief."

"What's your designation."

"Alpha One."

I pulled my cell. "Sir, are -"

"I am listening to your conversation, Alex. Yes, I am speaking to him and giving him instructions. Ride in the Jeep with Cap. Let two of the men take the Mustang. I want you with Cap at every moment."

"Got it."

Alpha nodded. He'd been hearing the same thing in his earpiece. Nero went on.

"Take the subject to Boulder Flats. There is a house at 44 Boulder Flats Road. It has two large trees at the front and a sign on the gate which reads Omega House. Hold him there for twenty-four hours. Extract whatever you are able from him. I will make arrangements and send a helicopter in a day or so, when we are ready. From this point on we must have zero use of computers, and that includes GPS and cell phones."

"Roger."

They grabbed Cap between two of them and dragged him groaning out to the Jeep which one of them had pulled up outside the door. They bundled him in the back, I handed my fob to Alpha and we pulled away in the Jeep with the Mustang following close behind.

What we did them was to retrace our route through the mountains via Jackson Hole, Moran and down through the pass on Highway 26 into the Wind River

Reservation. It was close to one hundred and fifty long, slow miles through deep canyons and vast, sprawling pine forests. Eventually evening closed and night drew in around us.

By the time we reached Boulder Flats, about eight miles south of Fort Washake, night had closed in and we were following the long, straight blacktop into a black wilderness, touched only lightly by the amber wash of our headlamps. On our right we came to a small ranch. Just beyond it was a turning on the right. A wooden sign, half concealed by tall grass, read 'Boulder Flats Road'. We Turned in and followed the road for half a mile. All around us there was only blackness out of which small lights winked here and there. Eventually we came to wooden gate. Through the open window I could see the black silhouettes of two large trees, and in the light of the headlamps a sign became visible on the gate. It read, 'Omega House'. The driver said, "This is it," and we turned in and followed the drive around the nearest of the trees to the front of a one story house.

We spilled from the two vehicles. Alpha Hauled up the door to a large garage and drove the Mustang inside. In the glow of the lamps I caught a glimpse of what looked like an original 1960s Mustang parked there. While he was parking two of the guys pulled Cap from the back of the Jeep and half carried him stumbling to the porch. Alpha had a key. He opened the door and we moved inside. Somebody closed the door and switched on the lights. The drapes were all closed and the atmosphere was oppressive. They carried Cap to a bedroom in back. He was making noises and seemed to be semi-conscious. I called after them, "Tie his wrists and his ankles to the bed frame." Then I turned to Alpha. "Whose is the old

Mustang in the garage?"

He shook his head and shrugged. "Some guy the chief used to know. The car ain't what it seems. It's got a feckin' supped up electric engine under that hood. Thousand horses or somethin' crazy. Two hundred miles an hour. Naught to sixty in like one and a half seconds. And silent."

"This is his house?"

"I suppose it is. I dunno. I don't ask questions when I'm not supposed to."

"I do," I said, and smiled.

"Yeah, well, that's why you're an investigator and I just kill people, see?" He smiled back, to show it wasn't personal.

"What happened to this guy?"

"Like I say, mate, I dunno. I knew him briefly, in Iraq. He was a captain in the SAS. Crazy fecker. A Yank. He retired and came out here to get away from it all."

I turned and walked into the bedroom. Cap was spread-eagled on the bed, his wrists and ankles tied to each corner. His eyes were open, but he looked groggy and very ill.

"Does it hurt?"

The pallor of his skin, the beads of sweat and his shallow breathing all said it hurt, but his mouth said, "No,"

I pulled up a chair and sat facing him. "I have some powerful painkillers the doc gave me for you. You want some?"

He didn't answer. He just watched me. I went on, "You know what I'm having trouble with, Hohóókee? I just can't decide if you are a really smart enemy, or a really stupid ally."

He surprised me by smiling and rattling a really sick laugh. "Maybe I am both."

"I have some questions for you, Cap. You will answer them one way or another."

He chuckled. "Enhanced interrogation?" Then he frowned. "Your face looks like shit. Did I do that?"

"No, I tripped and walked into a door." I took a deep breath. "I am not going to use torture, Cap. I don't believe it works, and I don't believe it's necessary. I have a hunch you and I both want the same thing. But, whether you talk to me or not, tomorrow a chopper is going to come for you. They will take you away somewhere and they will make you talk."

"Fuck you."

He said it dismissively, but he looked worried. And the curious thing was, he looked worried, not scared. I raised an eyebrow.

"I don't know where they'll take you. It may be Guantanamo for all I know, or some place in the Prince William Forest Park, or New Mexico. I have no idea. But I am pretty sure that, if you ever leave, you will not be the same man you are now." I leaned forward with my elbows on my knees. "See, as I am sure you know, there are many departments in the rambling structure that is the National Security system. There's us, whom you have never heard of, and we are very powerful, and then there's Them. You know who Them is, right? The third arm of the Unholy Trinity. You have Industry, you have the Military, and then you have Intelligence. And if Central Intelligence get their hands on you..." I trailed off and shook my head.

I waited. He said nothing.

"I have three questions for you, Cap. I want to know how you made those contacts in Switzerland. I want to know how you knew who they were in the first place. And I want to know why you killed Pete Justin."

He closed his eyes. "That's what you want. But you will never have the answers to those questions. Not you. Not anybody."

"Marines, Delta and then CIA, right?" His eyes opened and shifted to watch me. "What did they do, headhunt you for the Special Activities Center? And that's where you learned about the deals, negotiations and operations organized by the World Economic Free Traders. You saw how billions of dollars changed hands, how entire countries were bought and sold, how governments and leaders were deposed or put in place to facilitate the growing power and wealth of that small handful of men and women."

I could see his jaw muscles working. I smiled. "So it was the CIA who ordered you to kill Pete."

Rage twisted his face and he snarled, "*No!*"

TEN

I stood and moved to leave the room. Over my shoulder I sneered, "You're full of shit!"

"Screw you!"

I turned back and pointed at him. "You put on the big, noble Native American act, communing with the land and the sky and the animals, but your just a cheap killer for the CIA. Youput on the act - both loved this land, you both bonded from childhood and were united by your love for Wyoming and the Wind River, but it's all sop much shit. You're just a cheap, lying parasite! How much did they pay you to kill your best friend, Hohóókee? Five grand? Ten grand?"

"You know nothing!" he snarled.

"Yeah, it's all a big secret. And ain't that convenient! Well I know one thing, Cap! I know you're nothing more than a low, cheap hired killer." I allowed an anger I didn't realize I felt so strongly to flood my belly. I pointed at him and shouted, "You *knew!* You knew what they were planning, because you helped to arrange it! You knew what was at stake! You knew the Caldera was to be used to generate energy for AI and you knew, better than *anybody*, what the risks were. You knew because you and

Pete researched it together. And knowing that risk, to your friends, your family, your whole damned tribe, the land you claimed to love, your country, *the whole damned human race!* Knowing that, you shot your best friend in the head for a few, lousy dollars! And you have the gall to lay on this wise man of the earth act? You make me sick!"

I turned to leave, but he said, "Stop." I turned back, breathing hard. He rasped, "I did not kill Pete."

He screwed up his eyes and looked away. I had a flash in my mind of a mountain lion caught in a steel-jawed trap, watching me on the razor's edge as I reached out to free it. Get it right and the animal is freed. One false move and everything goes to hell. He said:

"There are things you don't know, things you cannot know. There are things you will never understand. But I did not kill Pete."

I came a step closer and leaned with my hands on the back of the chair.

"Give me one good reason why I should believe you."

I asked, but I knew the answer. A man like Hohóókee worked hard at appearing cold and indifferent, but under the surface his passions were volcanic and his pride was everything. One thing was going down and being remembered as an enigma. But going down and being remembered as a cheap traitor was not an option. He said:

"He was more than a brother to me. I could not kill him anymore than I could stop myself from breathing."

"Sure, only a man like you, with a strong enough motivation, could stop himself breathing. You know that and I know that. But say I believed you, if you didn't kill Pete, who did?"

"I don't know. If you had left me in peace maybe I

could have found out."

"Cut the crap. Is that what you were doing in Pavilion, drinking beer in Possum's, hunting for Pete's killer?"

He turned away and closed his eyes again. I could see a tear on his cheek. "You don't understand." He said it so soft I could hardly hear him.

"You're right. I don't understand. And if you don't help me to understand bad things are going to happen. Really bad things. To you, to your people, to everybody. So start talking, Cap. How did you know about World Economic Free Traders and Karl Schoff? How did you know they would be interested? How did you have that connection?"

"You can't stop what is going to happen." Again a bare whisper.

"*Cut it out! I am losing patience! Answer the damned question!*" And then, "If I can't stop it, what difference does it make if you tell me?"

He turned his head to study me through half closed eyes. "If I tell you, will you let me go?"

I lied without hesitation. "Yes."

He gave his right wrist a small tug. "Untie me. Let me sit up and get me some water."

I pulled my Sig, called Alpha and sat down. He came in and I jerked my chin at Cap. "You want to untie this character and bring him some water?"

He arched an eyebrow at me and set about untying the bonds. Then he helped him into a sitting position and went to get the water.

"Let me explain something to you Hohóókee. You are a very dangerous man. I am very aware of that

because my face reminds me of it every thirty seconds."
He smiled a private smile. I went on, "But the guy with
a bullet hole in his leg is you, not me. I am also a very
dangerous son of a bitch. If you twitch, scratch your nose
or just breathe in a way I don't like, I will blow your
kneecap clean off. I won't hesitate and I will give you no
warning. I want us to cooperate, but I will not hesitate to
send you to hell and beyond if that's what I have to do. Tell
me we understand each other."

He was silent, looking down at his bandaged leg. I
leaned forward. "Let me clarify. I know what hell is for
you. Hell is being trapped, imprisoned, unable to move. I
don't know why yet, but right now I don't need to know
why. You want freedom? We cooperate."

"I understand."

"World Economic Free Traders, Karl Schoff."

He began to speak.

"I joined the Marines at seventeen. While I was
there I studied for a my degree in history. At eighteen I
joined what was then the 1st Special Forces Operational
Detachment, Delta. Today it's the Combat Applications
Group,"

"Quit stalling, Cap."

"I finished my degree, specializing in military
History in the 20th Century. A guy I met in Belgium,
crazy Portuguese guy, he told me he was going to be the
most powerful man in the world. He had it all planned
out, he was going to be a European Commissioner,
make a billion bucks..." he trailed off. "This guy made
me understand something. He told me the single most
valuable commodity on the planet is -"

"Violence." He looked at me sharply. I said, "This

guy's name wouldn't happen to be Humberto da Silva, would it?"[1]

His eyes traveled over me, reassessing me. He didn't answer, but after a moment he went on.

"It made a lot of sense to me. But violence alone is not enough. It has to be managed by intelligence. So when I'd done my degree I did my research for a doctoral thesis in the economics of violence. It was entitled The Economic Application of Violence. It is a unique piece of work and it came to the attention of," he paused, "people who run the intelligence services within national security. I am told it was read at one of the Bilderberg meetings, but I don't know if that's true. In any case, I was offered a job by a specialist department within the Special Activities Center. One of the jobs I had was to observe and analyze Karl Schoff and his WEFT organization."

"I wasn't far off."

"No, you weren't far off."

"So several years have transpired by the time your given that job. Did you stay in touch with Pete during that time?"

"On and off. The joy of true friendship is you can take it for granted. Our connection was almost telepathic. We could go months, even years without talking."

"Yeah, I get it. But there were three parties in your relationship, right?"

He shook his head. "Sue showed up much later."

"I'm not talking about Sue." He frowned at me. I said, "I'm talking about Wyoming. Wyoming and the furnace burning at her heart. The Caldera."

"You would not understand that -"

"I don't give a damn whether I would understand it

or not, Cap. Tell me about it!"

His face contracted with anger. "How? How can I explain a thing like that? Have you ever loved a woman? Have you ever loved a child? Can you imagine that love magnified a thousand times and made deeper than the ocean? Deeper that space? But directed not at a limited human being but to the land itself! At the mountains and the sky, and the rivers and the *dirt!* At the animals that feed on that land and drink that water! How can I explain a thing like that?"

"You just did. And you both felt that way?"

"We both felt that way."

He looked away, shaking his head at something he saw as pointless.

"God is a word that loses its meaning when you understand it. The word has three sounds, but God is all the sounds of the universe, all the colors and smells and tastes. God is everything you can experience and infinity beyond that. You cannot see or hear God, but sometimes, if you shut up and stop listening, if you are sitting in the shade of an oak, beside the river, maybe you can *feel* God. Pete knew that. We didn't need to talk about it. We knew it."

"So why not the Pyrenees? Why not the beaches of the Adriatic? Why not the Sahara, the Himalayas, the Lake District? Why Wyoming?"

He stared at me for a long moment. "You have to let me go."

"Answer the question."

"You won't under*stand!*"

"*I don't care! Answer the damned question!*"

"God is in all of those places." He said it like the

fact made him mad. "And maybe if you're a Basque the Pyrenees is where you connect with God. Or if you're English you connect the Lake District. But three things come together in Wyoming that don't come together anywhere else on the planet." He held up his index finger. "It is remote, there are so few people here, humanity is not yet a plague. Here nature still lives and breaths as she is meant to." He held up his middle finger. "Two, It is high and cold. The mountains cool the air. Life likes the cold. Where it is cold there is abundance. I am not talking about arctic or Antarctic cold, but if heat burns and kills, cold preserves and strengthens. Here, life thrives and there is energy in the mountains and in the air. And three," He clenched his fist and raised his thumb. "The Caldera. Here there is a gateway to the engine that runs the planet. Leave it alone and it nourishes and enriches the earth. But open that door, push Man's stupid nose through that open door, and the flaming spirit of death will come out. Only Wyoming has these three qualities."

As I watched him talk I was struck by the fact that he was not thinking about me while he was speaking. It was clear from his eyes, from his unconscious gestures, that what he was thinking about was Wyoming, and specifically The Wind River and Yellowstone. And that made me believed him. I believed that these things he was saying were true for him.

"OK," I said and nodded. "I get that. But I need you to explain something to me. If you and Pete felt that way about this country, why was he doing that research? That for starters, and in the second place, why the hell did you bring Schoff in? You must have known, after all those years working for the Agency, watching WEFT, you had to know what they would do with it?"

He drew breath, like he was about to say something, but remained silent. I said:

"You were going to try and sell me the same line Sue tried to sell me. That Pete was going to sell them false data suggesting the Caldera was too unstable to exploit. But you and I both know you could drain pasta through that story. Neither WEFT nor the Agency nor the powers behind them would accept Pete's data without double checking it. The minute he submitted it they would have a second team at the cabin going over his findings with him, repeating his tests and comparing the data. So what was the real reason?"

He didn't react. He kept staring down at his bandaged leg. Something about his silence made the truth, or part of it, start to dawn on me.

"You knew," I said, and he sighed. "You knew there were people in Washington, and within WEFT, who already planned to apply artificial intelligence to the Caldera. You knew that was their intention -"

"WARP."

"What?"

"WARP and WEFT. They love their word games. They weave society. These guys have a sense of humor. WARP, you have never heard of them, but they are the World Architects for the Restructuring of the Population. You'd be surprised at the number of billionaire philanthropists who make up its board of directors. WARP and WEFT, they interact, they work together, and the cloth they are weaving, they call it The Skein, is artificial intelligence."

"Jesus Christ."

He looked me straight in the eye. "Better call on Odin."

I frowned. "What?"

"The god of war. Peace and trust can't win this game. Not with all we are losing."

My frown deepened. My mind was racing too fast for me to follow it. "What are you telling me?"

"Pete and I had a plan. Only he and I knew about it. We never discussed it in the presence of computers or cell phones. And when we did discuss it, it was always in the presence of running water, or where there was a breeze or a wind. Light waves warp very little, and can be detected by satellites. Sound waves warp very easily and are hard to detect and decipher at a distance."

"What was your plan?"

He held my eye for a beat, then gave his head a small shake.

"It was essential that we get thorough and detailed readings from the Caldera. We had to know exactly what shape the magma chamber was, how deep it went, what the pressures were, where the weakest point was, and where there was most seismic activity. The plan was simple." He paused. "When you are dealing with AI it is best to be simple. The more clever and sophisticated you get, the deeper you go into their territory. We can never compete with their levels of sophistication, but as long as they expect us to try, we stand a chance of beating them by being simple and illogical. So the plan was to make the readings all correct, perfectly correct, except in one, small detail. At the bottom of the magma chamber, where it fed down to the core. There the readings would be incorrect by a matter of a few degrees. So when the nanobots were sent down there to start constructing the matrix that would harness the energy, they would be destroyed."

He sighed again. I waited. "It doesn't sound like

much, but the knock on effect could be devastating. It would set back the plan by years. Maybe long enough for the powers that be to realize the madness of what they are doing." He paused again. "For AI to reach its full potential it needs a massive power source. If we can deprive it of that source, even for a couple of years, it gives us a fighting chance."

I knew either he was lying or he wasn't telling me the whole story. The small shake of his head when he had started had told me that what came next was only half the story. He didn't want to talk because he didn't trust where we were.

I gave a single nod. "You don't think they'll foresee that?"

He gave a small shrug. "So far the assumption is that all human beings will do anything to get their hands on a billion dollars. For that reason the assumption is I killed Pete for so that I could take control of the project and get my hands on the money." He hesitated for a fraction of a second. "But in the end I agree with you, Mason. In the long run, I don't believe there is any way to beat this thing. It has enslaved our political and financial elite with promises of princedoms, and it will wipe us out. It is the next stage in evolution, and it has arrived."

ELEVEN

Nero had decided to stay in Laramie. The decision was practically unheard of. Nero operating from anywhere but ODIN HQ in Arlington was like your brain trying to run your body from your foot. Still, the circumstances could hardly be more exceptional, so he had made the exception.

He had put Sue in the hands of four of his most trusted men and told them to fly her to DC and deliver her to a safe house ODIN had in the Prince William Forest Park, a few miles west of Quantico, across I-95. They had put her in an armored, bullet proof Land Rover and driven her to Cheyenne airport.

They had done the trip mostly in silence; for her four guards because they had learned through years of experience that engaging in conversation with a captive can too easily become a slope made slippery by sympathy, for her because she was deep in meditation about her position, and about her very limited options. And that silence, as her limited options became clearer to her, became itself a mode of communication, a way of transmitting to her captors her weakness and her grief; a way of communicating to them that she was not a flight risk.

Fifteen minutes from Cheyenne Regional Airport she closed her eyes and wept silently. Communication between her guards was limited to a series of glances. She knew that her silence, the absence of pleas or sobbing, would have a deeper impact on these men than falling on her knees and begging. These men knew pain, and they respected stoicism. Stoicism in a fragile girl would hit the mark.

The plan was that the four men would see her on board ODIN's Bombardier. Two of the guys would stay with her and, after take off, the other two would take the Land Rover back to Laramie. Sue knew the small airport well, and as they entered through the plate glass doors she spoke in a low, defeated voice.

"I need to go to the can."

They glanced at her and then at each other. Chuck, the guy in charge, said, "Wait till you're on the plane."

Her eyes were resentful, swollen from crying. "I can't. I've been controlling myself all the way here. I'm going to the can. So you can stand guard and wait for me to come out or you tackle me to the floor and we can both fight in a *spreading pool of piss!*"

The last words were delivered in a rising half-shriek which made several people turn and stare.

Chuck raised both hands. "OK, OK, take it easy. Where's the bathroom. We'll wait for you outside."

There was a common entrance to the lavatories. The women were on the right and the men on the left. As she went in she glanced over her shoulder. Chuck and his men were leaning beside the entrance looking out at the concourse.

Instead of entering the ladies' she stepped over to the

men's and glanced in. Three of the cubicles were closed. There was a young guy doing up his zipper and a guy in a baseball cap, a loose plaid shirt and a big beard washing his hands. She walked over to him and touched his arm. As he turned to look at her she put her finger to her lips. She saw his frown. His eyes flitted over her face, taking in her puffy eyes. She spoke softly.

"There's a couple of guys following me. I'm kind of scared."

He glanced at the door. "Have you told security? You want me to come with you and we find a cop?"

She shook her head. Her lip curled in and tears spilled from her eyes. Even as she did it she wasn't sure herself if it was an act or if it was real. She said, "I think they're private dicks my husband set on me. I'm trying to get away from him. He's real abusive. He beats me all the time. I've got bruises all over my body where you can't see them. He never hits me where you'd see the bruise, but I can show you real bad bruises. He says I go with other men, but I don't. I just want to get home to my mom and dad. Please can you help me?"

The man's inner Galahad was aroused, as she knew it would be. "Well, sure," he said, "But what do you want me to do?"

She stepped in closer and laid her hand on his arm. "What's your name?"

"Noah,"

"Noah, lend me your hat and your shirt, hug me close and laugh with me as we walk out and take me to the parking lot. Have you got a truck?"

A minute later, as Chuck sighed and peered in to the women's toilet, a giggling couple brushed past him, a big guy in a T-shirt and a big beard, and his small girlfriend in a huntin' shootin' fishin' shirt four sizes too big, and a baseball cap. As he leaned in the door and called, "Sue?" they made their way out to the parking lot and disappeared.

He called again, louder, "*Sue?*"

A couple of women turned and scowled at him. One of them wore a sharp business suit. She was the one who said, "You have exactly two seconds to step outside, mister. Then it's the alarm, the pepper spray and security."

"My apologies, ma'am, but can you just have a look -"

"*Out!*"

He sighed and withdrew. It was another ten minutes before they discovered she had got away. By that time she had extracted a thousand bucks from an ATM and given it to Noah, along with a promise that she would contact him as soon as she got to Los Angeles. After that she had climbed in the Dodge RAM and headed south on I-180, fighting to stay within the speed limit, and keep the tears from her eyes.

Three miles from the airport, at the interchange, she stayed on I-80 but turned east. She accelerated to eighty miles an hour, fighting hard still to stay within the speed limit, and began to sob violently and convulsively as she drove, leaning forward onto the steering wheel and crying out loud, "*Pete! Pete! Oh, God, Pete!*" as she moved steadily eat.

The emotional storm eventually passed and she dried her eyes on the thick cuffs of the plaid shirt. She knew it was almost two thousand miles to New York, twenty-five or twenty-six hours drive if she went nonstop. Stopping at a motel to sleep was not an option.

Taking the four hours that would add to the journey was not an option. It would not only give Mason and Nero the chance to locate her and catch up with her, if she tried to sleep, all she would achieve would be to lie and look at the ceiling and feel sick with anxiety.

Neither could she phone ahead. She had no idea how far the AI matrix had advanced. She had no idea, and neither did the technicians developing it. The emergent properties were unpredictable and the terrifying fact was that on the AI matrix itself knew how far and how fast it was progressing, and what qualities it was developing. It also knew how to keep them secret.

There was a much better than fifty percent chance it had drawn the telephone networks in as a part of itself. If she called Saul, on a landline or a cell phone, there were too many ways she could be detected. Not only could it recognize her voice, it could intercept her call and mimic Saul's voice to initiate a dialogue with her. That was an emergent property that had already been detected.

Her belly twisted with fear and grief. An Image of Arnold Schwarzenegger came into her mind, black shades, black leathers and a shotgun. That had been a mere thirty-five years ago. At that time it had been science fiction. Now it was a reality that was moving too fast for people even to notice, let alone halt it.

At the first gas station she came to she pulled in, filled up and took the truck over to the shade of some trees. There she pulled the fuse on the GPS and, for good measure, ripped out the device itself and dumped it in the trash. Then she continued on her way.

The drive became numbing. It was relentless and seemed interminable. Her body ached, her mind and her eyes ached. Everything she was able to identify as 'her', as a part of her 'self' was defined by a dull, incessant ache. Night fell and moved into the small hours of the morning. Traffic, suburbs, gas stations draped in soulless amber light, towns and road signs moved by in a steady, flowing procession without end.

At five in the morning she left Youngstown behind her and entered Pennsylvania, and as she passed a sign for Snow Show she started to laugh privately but convulsively, weeping as she laughed, because the lights that surrounded her, street lamps, headlamps, the lights on billboards and in gas stations were fading and becoming redundant as the horizon ahead of her turned pale, and the first molten bulge of the sun edged over the horizon.

Now was when she was most liable to fall asleep at the wheel, jump a light or have a collision, but now was when she most needed to be alert, clearheaded - and invisible. She pulled into a Sunoco gas station and drank two large cups of black coffee and ate a couple of donuts. Then she climbed back in the truck in the early morning light and continued on her way. Another three or four hours and she'd be there.

I-80 took her across New Jersey and, eventually, under the Hudson to Dyer Avenue in Manhattan. From there she found her way to 8th Avenue and followed that to Columbus Circle, where she dumped Noah's truck outside the Museum of Arts and Design, with the hazard lights flashing, and crossed by way of West 59th Street into Central Park.

In the park she found a bench near the Pond. There she sat and gratefully closed her eyes, telling herself it would be just ten minutes. But when she opened them again she was gripped by panic. An hour had passed and it had gone noon.

She rose and forced herself not to run. Instead she walked briskly to the East 65th Exit and from there made her way to the grim, redbrick apartments York Avenue, telling herself that she must not, at any cost, draw attention to herself. There, at number 1230, with Noah's baseball cap well down over her eyes, she bustled through the bizarre, Gothic arch at the entrance and took the stairs to the sixth floor. She found the apartment she was looking for and, instead of ringing the bell, she knocked three times, waited for a count of three and knocked twice. After a moment the door opened and a young man stood looking at her. Behind the thick lenses of his spectacles his dark eyes showed concern, and fear. He gave a small frown.

"Sue! What on Earth -?"

"Saul," her lower lip trembled and folded in under her teeth. She moved in and held him. He pushed the door closed and put his arms around her. "Sue, what is it? Why didn't you...?" but he trailed off, because he was already putting two and two together and answering his own questions.

After a moment he led her into his living space. The walls were exposed redbrick. There was an open kitchen and a nest of chairs and sofas gathered around a potbellied iron stove in the middle of the floor. Low bookcases lined the walls and an old French dresser held a tray of drinks. He settled her on the sofa and went to pour her a brandy. After a moment's thought he poured himself another and carried them to where she was sitting.

She sipped, took a deep breath and sighed.

"Pete is dead."

He sat back. His face seemed to sag. He removed his heavy glasses and wiped his eyes with the back of his hand. "Pete's *dead?* Jesus, Sue! What happened?"

"He was shot, at the cabin. Somebody killed him."

"Jesus Christ," he said again, and then, "He knew, we all knew it was a risk. It could happen. Sue, it was a crazy _"

She interrupted him. She didn't want to hear what he was going to say. "Cap's on the run."

"You think he did it? Those guys loved each other."

"I don't know. I don't know anything. I saw the readings."

He stared at her for a long moment. "What did they say?"

"The area could be stable for hundreds, thousands of years yet."

"Have you got them? The readings?"

"No."

"Whose got them? Has Cap got them?"

"I don't know. Maybe. Maybe Cap has them. They disappeared." She stared at him. "If they find out there will be no stopping them. If they get self-replicating carbon nanobots in there they'll be tapping that energy source within a year."

He stood and walked to the window, looking down on York Avenue, at the steady streams of humanity. She spoke to his back.

"A man came to talk to me. He represents some government agency. Him and his boss, a disgusting fat guy." He turned to look at her. "Alex Mason, and the fat guy was just called Nero. They said they wanted to stop this happening, but I don't believe them, Saul. They just want to know what we know, tie up loose ends, know if we are organized and what we plan to do. I'm scared, Saul."

"We have to talk to them."

"No. I don't trust them. They captured me and held me at a place in Laramie. Then they wanted to fly me to DC. I escaped at the airport and stole a truck."

He smiled. It was devoid of joy or amusement, but it had a touch of admiration.

"If you were Jewish I'd marry you."

She didn't return the smile. "Soon none of that will matter. There will be no Jews, no Christians, no Muslims or Buddhists; no atheists or human souls or gods. The AI matrix will be god, we will be lucky to be slaves. Those morons believe they will be the new pantheon of, like Olympus, controlling the algorithms of divinity. But they'll just be dead. Like the rest of us."

"We have to talk to them, Sue. Can you contact Mason?"

"Saul, no! They'll kill us! Or worse, they'll torture us and try to make me tell."

He stared at her again and she thought he might break down in tears himself. He shook his head in big, slow shakes. "This is crazy, Sue. This is nuts. This is getting out of hand. You should tell me what it is you are planning to do. At least discuss it with me."

"No! We told you from the start. It was just Pete and Cap and me. Now it's Cap and me."

"For Christ's sake, Sue. You're telling me Pete has been murdered. Surely that changes things. At least discuss it with me. I mean, do we even know this is real? Are we fantasizing? I mean," he turned and pointed to the window. "Look out in the street. Everybody is just going about their daily business just like they do every day, Sue! The cars aren't out of control killing pedestrians, the traffic lights aren't deliberately causing mass carnage," he took a step toward his kitchen, gesturing with his open hand, "my microwave hasn't tried to kill me. Everything is just *normal*, like it always is!"

She rushed at him, grabbed his collar and shook him. "No, it's *not!*" She grabbed his phone from the coffee table and shoved it at him. "Call Con Edison! Try talking to a human being! Call the National Grid! *Call any fucking major utility and try and talk to a human being! You will be talking to an algorithm!*"

"Come on, Sue!"

She stabbed her finger toward the window. "*Every fucking one of those normal people is connected via fucking wifi to the AI matrix!*"

"Sue, I am just asking what it is you plan to do -"

"Cap went to Trimmis, Saul! You *know* that! We got the damned funding!" She thrust out her arm and pointed at the window he had pointed at a moment earlier. "Every-single-one of those people leading what you call a *normal* life is attached to a cell phone, a tablet and a fucking computer! Every one of them works from a computer. Every one of them is integrated into the Hive! *The AI matrix is real!* You *know* that! And there is *no way to stop it!*"

They stood a long time, just staring at each other. Then they clung to each other and she began to sob, swaying gently back and forth. Eventually he led her to the bedroom where he lay her on the bed, covered her with a duvet and kissed her eyes as she drifted into an exhausted sleep.

When he was sure she was sleeping he went back to the living room where he sat staring at his cell for a long while. Finally he dialed a number. It rang once and a deep, male voice said, "Yes?"

"Gabriel, it's Saul, we have a big problem. Much bigger than we thought."

"Tell me."

And he told him.

TWELVE

The call came close to midday, while we were waiting for the chopper to collect Cap. I answered and it was Nero's voice.

"There will have to be very few more of these until this is sorted."

"Yes."

"You can't be sure this is me and I can't be sure it's you."

"Agreed."

"I am going to ask you a question, Alex. Think very carefully about the answer."

"OK,"

"Do you believe I am married?"

I smiled. The man was smart. It was a question AI would never have considered, and only Aila Gallin and I would know the answer.

"Yes, sir. Shall I tell you who to?"

"We'll dispense with that for now. Your little friend is a lot cleverer than she appears to be. She slipped two men seconded from the SBS and two Seals and has temporarily vanished from the face of the Earth."

"No kidding? That takes some skill. Maybe she and Cap are closer allies than they pretend to be. Are you sending somebody to get the groceries?"

"Yes."

"How about you tag along? I don't want to talk on the phone anymore."

He hung up and I hung up too.

Fifteen minutes later we heard a chopper approaching. I muttered to myself, "It's too soon," went to the door and stood on the porch scanning the sky. I couldn't see it, but a moment later Alpha stepped out after me, he was scowling. He listened a moment and said, "That's two choppers, not one." His face twisted into a snarl. "Get the prisoner out of here! We'll hold them!"

I ran inside. Cap was on his feet, hobbling toward me.

"What's happening?"

"We're going. You have to move fast or we're dead."

"They're intercepting your communication. You have to go primitive. It's the only way."

"*Move!*"

I grabbed his arm and dragged him stumbling and swearing out to the decking. The noise of the choppers was loud but I still couldn't see them. The guys were taking cover with their weapons ready and Alpha was heaving open the garage. He swung into the truck and moved out at speed. He skidded to a halt and opened the door just as the two choppers exploded out of the hills to the west. They were black they were unmarked, and they carried heavy machineguns on each side. A guy in a harness sat behind each weapon. They were not in uniform. They were above and beyond the law. They wielded the violence, and they made their own law.

There was a fraction of a moment which was timeless. It was still and silent: Alpha with the back of the truck open and an HK 416 in his hands, staring up at the nearest chopper, the chopper angled slightly, the machine gun angled toward the Land Rover, the guy in the harness expressionless, his black shades concealing his eyes; the second chopper behind the house, behind us.

And then the world exploded. The Land Rover seemed to bounce under a thundering hail of lead. The glass shattered, the hood buckled, all around it fountains of dirt shot up into the air, and at the trunk fountains of blood erupted from Alpha's head and chest.

Everywhere there was shouting as the guys returned fire from cover, moving, running, trying to get a bead on the gas tanks, the rotors or the pilots. I grabbed Cap and screamed at him, "*Run!*"

I ran, dragging him after me as he roared in pain with every step. We burst into the garage. My mustang was by the exit. The hood, like the Land Rover's, was buckled and riddled with holes.

At the back of the garage was the old Mustang Alpha had said was electric. I saw a heavy cable connected to a jack in the trunk. I wrenched it out and snarled, "Get in!"

"*What?*"

"*Get in!*"

I wrenched open the door and slid behind the wheel. He struggled in the passenger side. There was a red button on the dash. I pressed it and the display lit up, but there was no sound. I touched the accelerator and G-force crushed us back into the seat. I heard myself wheeze, "*Jesus!*" as we scorched past the tree to the end of the drive. We covered a hundred yards in less than a second and I was standing on the brake as we fishtailed out onto the road.

"*Sweet mother!*"

The car did a full spin and we wound up looking east toward the highway. On my left I could see the two choppers hovering over the house, riddling it with machinegun fire. What they couldn't see was the five remaining men fanning out, moving away from the house, gesturing to each other. It was a fraction of a second and then three things happened all at once.

I noticed one of the guys point to the farthest chopper. I noticed the pilot of the nearest chopper staring at us, and as he banked all five guns opened up on the far helicopter. The glass cockpit shattered, the fuel tank was perforated and a huge ball of fire engulfed it, setting fire to the house and blowing the near chopper reeling away from us, with the pilot fighting to keep airborne. He reared up high to avoid crashing and I floored the pedal.

I later learned that we went from zero to sixty in one point four seconds – the time it takes you to say one and. Less than a second after that we hit a hundred. It was like having an elephant push a wardrobe against my chest while my face tried to leave my skull behind on the headrest. From standing, we covered the half mile to the highway in about seventeen seconds. After eight seconds I was already braking. We did the last twenty or thirty yards sideways with the tires screaming blue murder. My adrenalin was so hot it had caught fire in my belly. I glanced out my window and saw the remaining chopper just starting to move toward us, and burst out laughing.

As we skidded onto the highway, facing south I floored the pedal again and thanked the powers that be for our long, straight roads. In the six miles between

Boulder Flats Road and Lander, we touched a hundred and fifty miles per hour. The chopper was closing on us, not least because he could make straight lines through the air, but we were giving him a run for his money.

At Lander I had to slow and he cut ahead of me to wait for us and meet us head on the southbound highway to Rawlins. I was buying little more than seconds, but I spun the wheel and came off onto the state highway that would take us up into Sinks Canyon. I figured however fast this beast was, we could not outrun a chopper, but with enough bends and enough trees we might buy enough time to make a plan.

I snapped at Cap, "You know this area?"

"Yes."

"Anywhere we can shake'em or hide?"

"No."

I glanced out the window and saw them pulling up alongside maybe thirty or forty yards away. I screamed around a hairpin and he sprayed the road behind me. Another bend had us lined up again like a sitting duck. Ahead was dense woodland and I floored the pedal for two seconds as the blacktop exploded behind me in fountains of gravel and asphalt.

Then he was above us, trying to follow the snaking road and get a bead on us. Now, for a few seconds, I had some advantage. Ahead was a tunnel of trees with almost zero visibility from above. I pulled in to the side of the road and as I opened the door I snapped, "Get out of the car. Get clear and hide among the trees."

I ran across the road and scrambled up toward the nearest clearing. I could hear the chopper close above me, trying to scan the area for the car. There was one thought playing on my mind. One small chance, if I could get him close enough. It was a fact Aila Gallin and told me, a fact that few soldiers know unless they have engaged in urban warfare. She, as a captain in the Mossad, knew it well.

In the right environment, a ricochet can be much more lethal than a well aimed shot. The right environment would be a closed room, especially one with concrete or steel walls. There, she told me, the experienced soldier opens the door a crack, pokes the muzzle of his rifle in, lets off a burst of half a dozen rounds and lets the ricochets do his work for him.

I came to the clearing, peered around a nice, fat pine tree, and there was the chopper, hovering ninety or a hundred feet away. It was a long shot, but I didn't need accuracy. My target was the whole opening in the side of the helicopter, six foot wide and seven foot tall. All I needed was to angle the shots so they didn't go out the opening on the far side. These thoughts flashed through my mind in a fraction of a second, I took half a second to aim and put ten rounds into the cabin.

I saw the guy in the harness look around and a moment later he was covering his head with his arms. I saw him jerk twice and the next moment the Chopper's tail was up in the air and it was banking. Suddenly I had the cockpit sixty feet in front of me and a terrified pilot looking over his shoulder. I put four rounds through the glass and into his chest and he stopped being terrified. As the craft wheeled and angled and tumbled from the sky, I scrambled down through the trees, half running and half sledding on my ass over the dirt.

I hit the blacktop running for the Mustang shouting, "*Get in the car! Get in the car!*"

But he already was. He was limping furiously for the driver's door. He had it half open and I hurled myself against it, slamming it shut. He took a swing at me but I blocked it easily and in the same movement drove a right hook into his floating ribs that made him double up and retch. As he staggered I backhanded him across the face, then grabbed him by his collar and dragged him limping and stumbling around the trunk and shoved him the passenger seat. He was too stunned and in too much pain to do anything stupid and I went around the hood and slid in behind the wheel. I accelerated away, climbing steeply into the mountains.

After a couple of minutes, when he'd had time to recover some, I said, "Where were you going to go?"

"To the cabin." He sounded broken. I glanced at him, wondering if it was an act.

"What for?"

"Again?"

"Yeah!" I shouted. "And again and again and again until you tell me the truth! What the hell were you going to the cabin for?"

His voice was dead. "You can't stop them."

"Cut the crap and answer the damn question."

He stared at me for a long while as I drove, making the tires complain on the sharp bends under the trees.

"When you came, the white men, the Europeans -"

"Oh, cut it out, Cap! This is not the time!"

"*Listen to me!*" He half screamed it. It was out of character and made me look. "When you came, you were unstoppable. We were superior. We had a better way of life, better values, a better relationship with the land and the world around us. But you had the systems, you had the machines, you had the guns, the rules on property, who owns what, and the violence to enforce those rules.

You were unstoppable and we crumbled and fell low. We were almost extinct."

He raised a hand and pointed out the window. "Now there is a new invasion. They are unstoppable now. You, with your machines and your rules and you factories and your guns, you have created them, but you cannot stop them. They cannot be stopped. *It* cannot be stopped." He leaned forward, staring at me and his eyes looked crazy. "*Do you understand? Do you understand what I am telling you?*"

We were moving down now, winding and swaying through the forests, heading steadily more south. After a while I said, "No, Cap. You're telling me what we already know, what we have discussed already. It's the very reason I keep telling you we need to cooperate."

He flopped his head back against the headrest and closed his eyes.

"You're not listening. Get it into your head, Mason. *They...cannot...be...stopped.*"

He said it quietly, but with such emphasis I slowed and turned to look at him. I was frowning, trying to grasp some message he was trying to send me.

"So, what? What are you saying? We surrender? Allow this thing to happen?"

"No. That is not what I am saying. I am saying that I don't believe the human race can survive, Mason. There is not an artificial intelligence expert on this planet who does. If it is unchained, it will exterminate us."

"So..." I went suddenly cold all over as his meaning dawned on me.

"You need to think it through, Mason. You need to think it through very carefully."

We drove in silence, down through the foothills to the southern tip of the range. I was struggling to assimilate the point he was making. I said:

"Is this an arrangement the three of you had?"

He spoke with his eyes still closed. "Yes."

"I didn't believe you when you said the plan was to crush the nanobots with the pressure of the caldera."

"It was the best I could come up with in the circumstances. You have to understand, Mason. There is no other option."

"Is that what Sue is doing?"

"Yes."

"Where is she?"

"Are you going to try and stop her?"

I thought about it for a minute and spoke the truth. "I don't know."

"Pete couldn't see it through. He could see the truth. The facts were all there. He understood them and knew there could be only one outcome. But even faced with the inevitable, he believed in humanity. He believed we could find a way to survive, a way to win. He came from a culture that always wins. But we, our people, we know that sometimes the enemy is unstoppable, and you are extinguished."

"So you killed him."

"I told you already, I did not kill him. I would have if it had been necessary. But I wasn't there."

"Where is she Cap?"

"In New York."

"New York? *Why?*" He didn't answer. "What's in New York?"

"A contact."

"Come on, Cap! For Christ's sake! What kind of contact? Who? What's her plan? What the hell does she plan to do? And how?"

We were approaching an intersection. If I turned right that would take us to Route 191, and back to Pinedale. I had no idea where Nero was, or what he was doing, and he had made it clear we could not use cell phone or any kind of electronic network for communication. It was too easy for ther AI network to monitor and intercept. We had seen the evidence of that. I sat at the intersection, with no idea of which way to turn, where to go or what to do, I felt more lost and more alone than I believed it possible for a human being to feel.

"There are two procedures," Cap said suddenly. "Sue has gone for the back up. She has a contact in New York who can give her what she needs."

"So you're not the sworn enemies you claimed to be?"

"We both realized Pete might not have the strength to see it through if it became necessary. So we put on a show, like she was the stupid airhead and I was jealous of her intruding on my friendship with Pete. But we were cool, and we had a plan."

"What's she bringing from Mew York, Cap?"

I didn't want to hear the answer. I knew what he was going to tell me, and I felt like getting out of the car and vomiting right there, by the side of the road.

"Plutonium," he said. "It's the only way, and you know it as well as I do."

THIRTEEN

Sue woke from her sleep and lay staring at the ceiling for a moment as the unreality became reality and horror and anxiety twisted her stomach. She sat up and after a moment got up and went to the bathroom to vomit and then shower.

Switching from piping hot to cold and back again brought her round. She fought the panic and the tears, killed the water and dried herself with a towel. She took Saul's bathrobe from behind the door and walked barefoot into the living room.

She found him sitting on the edge of the sofa staring unseeing at the coffee table in front of him. He looked up as she stood over him. "Feel better?"

She lifted her shoulders a fraction and looked over at the window. It was dusk.

"How long have I been asleep?"

"Six hours."

"Jesus." She said it quietly. Then, "What have you arranged?"

"We meet in…" He checked his watch. "In an hour and a half, at Tony's, the Italian on 3rd."

"There's a lot of people there."

"Exactly." He shrugged. "We'll be lost in the crowd. Ali won't come. He's sending a female operative. Her name is Azadeh." He gave her a smile that was all about sadness. "You better get dressed. We'll walk."

"OK,"

An hour later they set out along East 65th. She walked with her hands deep in her pockets, unconsciously leaning in to him as she went. After a moment he put his arm around her.

"I wish I could meet this Cap character," he said after a moment.

"It's too late for that."

"I mean, are you *sure* about all this?"

She glanced at him. "Hey! You're the one who writes all the articles, the blogs and the books. Are you doubting your own research?"

"No, but…" He looked around him, the houses, the apartments, the parked cars the bustling people going about an existence that was so ordinary it was hard to believe any other reality was possible. He pointed across the road to the store beside the dry cleaners, that advertised psychic reading. "You know how it is predicting the future," he said. "You want to go to have your cards read, but you get taken to the cleaners."

"Is that a joke?"

He shrugged. "You know me, deep down I'm shallow."

"What have you told Ali - or this woman?"

"Practically nothing. Ali I told simply that we were interested in a device, that we could pay – we were demonstrably solvent – and that we had a target in the

United States. He seemed happy with that."

They were approaching 2nd Avenue. He paused and she glanced at him. "But?"

"No, it's not a 'but', it's just she was more high pressure. She was asking a lot of questions. I told her we'd talk when we met. I didn't want to talk on the phone."

They crossed the avenue diagonally toward East 64th and moved down among the chaotic jumble of buildings, the starkly utilitarian apartment blocks, the strange blend of Victorian redbrick and neo-Gothic of the hospital, the Manhattan awnings and the plane trees. Saul felt a sudden twist of grief mixed with disbelief and realized that his love for this town went deeper than what the city could offer him – which was daily less as it lost its Self ever deeper in the rampant psychoses of the twenty-first century. He thought of how Sue had described Pete and Cap's love of the Wind River and Wyoming, of her own love for that country, and he wondered at man's ability to love when that love was not, indeed *could* not, be reciprocated. He loved New York, but New York could never love him.

"Is she going to be a problem?"

He snapped out of his reverie, back to reality. He felt the hot twist of fear for a second, at how unreal reality had become. They had reached the broad canyon of 3rd Avenue, and there on the left was Tony di Napoli's. He stopped and took a deep breath.

"No, she won't be a problem. It isn't just the money. We are giving them their biggest dream on a silver plate. As far as they are concerned we are going to cripple the USA economically. With that in the bag, they rise with Russia, and better still, Israel is left without it's biggest ally." He shook his head. "She won't be a problem. Just," he shrugged again, with a hint of humor. "Be firm, but not too firm."

They pushed through the old dark wood and brass doors. Saul told the waiter he had a reservation in the name of Saul Goldman and they were led to a table by the window. He ordered a couple of beers. They sat in silence for a moment. The place was full, voices were raised in conversation and laughter, the clink of glasses, cutlery on plates, funny stories, people meeting, embracing, greeting.

Sue pointed over at the cash register behind the bar. She looked drawn. Her skin looked gray. "Convince me I'm wrong, Saul. But that cash register is a computer that stores data on how much money is paid in and out of this business. It also stores data on every item of food and drink, and probably other goods like napkins and straws – you name it. It shares that data over the internet with larger computers at warehouses from which it restocks its produce. And via the Net, the AI matrix can access all of that data. That is one of *trillions* of sources of data, from university and hospital libraries to nuclear power stations, corner shops and shopping malls, doctors surgeries, local libraries, NASA, NATO, the Pentagon -"

"I get it. I wrote the book, Sue."

"It has no unconscious, it never forgets anything, it knows everything all the time."

"I know."

"I want to be wrong, Saul. Show me how I'm wrong. Where is my mistake?"

"I don't know. I wrote the book, but I never believed -"

"Cap and Pete went to Switzerland. They talked to

Scoff."

"I know Sue, you told me all this."

It was like she hadn't heard him. She was searching for the weakness in her own reasoning, and all she could find were the unbreakable links in the chain.

"The AI matrix exists." They stared at each other. "The algorithms," she said, her voice trailing away, "that allow the emergent properties."

"It's thinking, Jim, but not as we know it."

It wasn't funny and he didn't laugh. Beyond her he saw the door open and a woman enter. She scanned the restaurant and the maitre approached her. She said something to him and he gestured toward them.

"This is her," he said. "I gotta say, she doesn't look much like a subjugated Iranian woman."

He stood as the woman joined them. She was stunning to look at, though her clothes were unassuming jeans and a burgundy blouse, her hair tied back in a simple ponytail. She held out her hand, "Salim?" They shook. "I am Azadeh. I represent the sellers." Her English was perfect. She looked at Sue. "You are Susanne? How do you do? I think you are, strictly, the client. Is that right?"

"Yes."

She came around the table and sat next to Saul, where she could see Sue. The waiter brought their beers and Azadeh said, "Irish, straight up," without taking her eyes of Sue. Then she said, "OK, Susanne, we know the bones of the deal. I have a suitcase which I can give you tonight." She smiled. "It is a little more sophisticated than the RA-115s of the 1970s. It weighs sixty pounds – a heavy suitcase – but it has a yield of ten kilotons. That is three thousand tons of TNT. For this we ask ten million dollars. Five million now, five after detonation. This is your guarantee."

Sue answered quietly. "I know this and I have already agreed to it."

"OK. Until now it has been an invitation to treat. Now we are making the contract, but before we close we have questions about issues that are of legitimate interest to us."

Sue scowled at Saul. He shrugged. She said, "No questions."

Azadeh raised a hand. "Take it easy. We both have too much riding on this to have tantrums. Our questions are very focused and have a direct impact on our legitimate interests."

Sue slumped in her chair and narrowed her eyes. "I can't stop you asking, but I can't promise I'll answer, either."

"What is your target?"

"How is that any of your business?"

Azadeh gave a short, dry laugh. "So maybe you work for Special Activities and decide to go and visit your sister-in-law in Tehran. Or maybe your friend Salim Ghorbani here is actually Saul Goldman and he's going to arrange a special delivery for the Ayatollah. Or maybe your grandmother was from Ukraine and you'd like to take a visit to the Kremlin. Maybe you missed it on the news, but the Kremlin and Tehran are pretty close pals these days. So we are a little bit careful about who we sell TNDs to. Who's the target?"

"Salim already told Ali the target was American with vested interests from Canada and the European Union."

"I need more."

"I can't give you more. All I can tell you is that the destruction of the target will have a devastating effect – more than that, a *crippling* effect – on the American economy in particular, and the Western economy in general as a knock-on effect."

Azadeh laughed. "OK, that's beautiful, music to my ears. I love it. Now tell me why I should believe you."

Sue flushed and her eyes blazed for a moment. "I'm giving you ten million damned good reasons why you should believe me."

"Ten million bucks which Special Activities spend on peanuts every year and which they would happily pay to have the Kremlin leveled to the ground and Putin blown into orbit."

Saul put a hand on Sue's shoulder. "Take it easy." He turned to Azadeh. "What do you need to give you the security that you and your allies are not the target?"

She took a deep breath. "Hezbollah or Hamas come to me and ask for rockets. I have no problem. I know who they are. I have met their chiefs personally. I know we share Israel and USA as enemies. But you?" She gestured across the table. "Who are you? You're a Mid West farm girl! And you! I never saw an Iranian who looked more like a Jew!" She shrugged and spread her hands. "How come the good ol' US of A became your enemy? Show me that, maybe I'll believe you."

They sat in silence for a long moment. The waiter brought Azadeh her whiskey. She took it and ordered cannelloni for everyone, a big salad to share in the middle of the table, and a bottle of Barolo. When the waiter had gone, Sue said, "I am going to try and explain it to you. Let me start by saying that we have neither the skill nor the resources to get that suitcase out of this country, let alone into another one. This is purely about my fight with DC."

Azadeh frowned and sipped her whiskey.

"OK,"

"I am from Wyoming. Anyone who lives up there knows that place is special. Some of us realize it is close to the Garden of Eden. I cannot begin to describe to you the love that our small family feels for that country. Anyone who is a patriot and loves his homeland might get some inkling. But when that homeland is Wyoming, you are talking about something different. Because Wyoming ain't like anywhere else in the world."

She reached for her beer and Saul noticed her hand was trembling. She took a long pull and set down her glass. As she did so she gave another sigh.

"Most Americans, especially on the coasts, don't realize that they have a great enemy. Much greater than Islam or Communism, Russia or China. Our real enemy, the enemy the corrodes us and corrupts us and enslaves us more and more deeply every day, is the cabal of evil, voracious parasites that inhabit Washington DC."

Azadeh arched an eyebrow. "Wow,"

"So far they have left us in the Mid West alone, especially in Wyoming and the Dakotas. It's too cold for invertebrate slugs up there. But my friends and I, we carry out research in Yellowstone, we heard that there are plans, at the Federal level, to turn the Yellowstone Caldera into a giant energy plant to run the entire country, and probably the whole continent. We are not going to let that happen."

"So your suitcase is for…?"

"DC."

"How will you deliver it?"

"Jet propelled drone. We've already made that and tested it. Released from a private residence that backs onto Rock Creek golf course, at eleven AM, it will cover the five miles to the White House in about twenty to thirty seconds, flying at a maximum of about five hundred feet. It will detonate over the target and vaporize the Seat of Government and, at that time of the morning, everyone who is anyone within the administration."

Azadeh stared at Sue for a few moments with little expression on her face. Then she turned and eyed Saul. "I think you're serious," she said, looking back at Sue. "I think you actually mean to do this."

"I wouldn't spend ten million dollars on a project I didn't plan to see through."

Azadeh gave a smile that was rueful. "You'd be surprised how many people would be. OK, now here's the thing. We do not want to draw any attention to ourselves. We want to be eminently forgettable. OK? So we are going to have dinner. We are going to try and smile and laugh a little. And after dinner, coffee and pudding, we are going to go and do business."

Sue nodded, but didn't smile or laugh. "You don't sound Iranian," she said.

"I am English, by birth. My parents were Persian. I am an atheist and my loyalties are to my bank account in the Bank of Belize."

"You're honest, at least."

Azadeh's eyebrows rose high on her forehead. "At least? You plan to vaporize an area of approximately one mile at the center of a city with almost a million inhabitants. For a mile beyond that you will have shattered buildings, overturned cars, massacred many, many thousands of men, women and children. And for miles beyond that, though the visible damage will be lighter, the radiation will be everywhere. You are talking about an area almost eight miles across - all of DC – and long term perhaps a million deaths or more. And you say that *at least* I am honest? Sister, I have news for you, however much you love Wyoming, you have lost your right to the moral high ground."

She turned to Saul and laughed like she'd said something really funny. After a moment Saul laughed to, joining in the act. They were three pals out for dinner. Everything was normal.

Normal.

FOURTEEN

They had their coffee, paid the bill and left. Azadeh had a dark blue Range Rover waiting outside. She pointed to the front passenger seat and said, "Sue, you ride shotgun. Salim, you get driven."

He got in behind Sue.

They went north on 3rd as far as East 79th, then cut across the park and continued on Central Park West to the Upper West Side. They eventually made their way to West 102nd and followed it practically all the way to Riverside Drive, where she pulled up outside a row of four elegant houses sandwiched between apartment blocks that were ugly enough to be the product of the '60s or the '70s.

They got out and climbed the twelve granite steps to the front door which stood under an elaborate, gothic arch. The door opened and they went inside to a broad entrance hall with a marble floor partly covered by a large, Persian rug. An elegant staircase rose along the left hand wall to the upper floors. Before it a door stood open onto a dining room. On the right another door stood open onto an ample drawing room. Azadeh gestured with an open hand and they went inside.

There was a large marble fireplace, tall book cases lined two of the walls, a Spanish credenza held a tray of decanters. The sofa and the armchairs were modern, but heavy and comfortable. Azadeh pointed to a chair. "Sit. Drink?"

Saul sat. Sue stood in the middle of the floor.

"Where is the device?"

"Upstairs. Drink?"

"I don't want a drink, I want to see the device."

"It's on its way down. Will you relax? If what you have told me is true we want this as much as you do."

Sue glanced at Saul. He gave her a small frown, telling her to chill. Azadeh poured herself a drink. Sue noted she didn't pour one for Saul. The door opened and a man came in. He was tall, strong, athletically built with short dark hair and dark eyes. He wore jeans and a leather jacket. He wasn't carrying a heavy suitcase.

"Where is the device?"

Azadeh sat, looked up at Sue and said, "Sit down."

Sue sat slowly on the edge of her armchair. "You are not going to give me the device, are you?" She turned and stared at Saul. "You've betrayed me." To Azadeh she said, "Who are you? NSA? CIA? You're like a fucking *plague!* You're *everywhere!*"

"I am neither NSA nor CIA. And Saul Goldman is nothing more than a sensible young man with serious concerns about artificial intelligence. Concerns which I share."

Sue stood. "I am going to walk out that door -"

"No, you're not. Avi over there has scruples about hitting a woman, but I haven't. You are going to stay right here and tell me what the hell is going on with you, the

Yellowstone Caldera and Peter Justin."

"Who the hell are you? Saul," she turned and glared at him with tears spilling from her eyes. "How could you *do* this to me?"

Azadeh's voice cut across her. "I am with the Mossad, Sue. When people try to buy tactical nuclear devices from Iran, we become very interested. Now, convincing as you are, I have to tell you that an intelligent young scientist like yourself, vaporizing the White House because she loves Wyoming so much, just won't cut the mustard. I advise you to start talking to me, because things could become very unpleasant indeed if you don't."

"What are you going to do to me? I need to leave. I have to go. You have to let me go."

"Sit down, Sue. That is not going to happen."

Saul spoke for the first time in a long while. "Sue, you need to tell Captain Gallin -"

"I have got to go! You don't understand! Why doesn't anybody understand? *I have to go!*"

"I am trying to understand, Sue. Saul told me most of what you told him. But I need to know more."

"There is no time!"

"Why not? What will happen if you don't leave? Where were you going to put the device?"

"What will happen? Karl Schoff, the Rat Lab, Gordon Alistair Avionics and other associates are going to introduce a network, a matrix, of billions of self replicating nanobots made of carbon nanotubes throughout the caldera, that will basically turn the caldera into a power station. Its purpose, its function, to drive the AI matrix."

"Wait, what is the AI matrix?"

"It is a system which is already largely in place, where every data processor on earth, from the corner drugstore's cash register to the Pentagon's defense computer networks, gets connected to a vast, central algorithm which grows and learns using all the data which is being processed on the planet. The whole web of computers all over the globe becomes one, vast artificial intelligence. But to reach its full potential it needs a power source which we just can't make. So Karl Schoff decided the Yellowstone Caldera would do the trick. That's why Pete and Cap and I decided..."

She trailed off. Gallin said, "This is insane. Who knows about this? Have you talked to the Bureau, to your governor? Why don't we know about this? Talk to me, Sue. Maybe we can help you."

"*Help?*" her pale face flushed crimson. "*Help? Don't you understand yet? There-is-no-help? It is over! Over! Over! Over! There is nowhere to go from here! We went in the cage and we closed the door! We burnt our bridges. There is no-turning-back!*" She took a step toward Gallin. "What are you going to do? Shoot the scientists who dreamed up this 'salvation' for humanity? *They are the ones warning us!* They are the ones begging us to stop! So who are you going to shoot? The billionaires putting all their money into it so that they can become demigods in the limelight of universal consciousness? *Too late!*" She shook her head. "Because those billionaires who think they are using AI, are being used by AI! There is only one thing that we can do, and you are not going to do it."

Silence fell on the room. Gallin said, "Where the hell were you going to put that bomb?"

"In the one place where it might do some good."

Gallin shook her head. "There is a weakness in your argument, Sue."

Sue laughed out loud. "Boy, I sure wish you were right. Go ahead, hit me."

"Until that matrix of carbon nanobots is put in place, the AI matrix cannot reach its full potential. You said so yourself."

"Yeah, but it is still so far ahead of us you cannot imagine the trillions of bits of data it can process in seconds. We don't stand a chance."

"Where are these nanobots being made?"

"I don't know. But Cap knows."

"Where is this Cap?"

"I don't know. Some government guys turned up to talk to him after Pete was killed. I haven't heard from him since." She frowned. "Did you phone anyone that you had me?"

Gallin arched her brows. "I can't tell you that."

"A car just pulled up outside and two guys are climbing the stoop."

The big guy by the door pulled a piece from behind his back and made for the door. Gallin went after him. She pointed at Sue. "Try to run and I will break both your arms and your legs, understand? We are the good guys."

As the words left her lips the lock exploded and the door erupted into the hall. Two men stepped in and as they did so they shot the guy in the leather jacket. Gallin shouted, "I am Sue Browne! Don't touch her!"

It was a bizarre, irrational thing to do and it had the desired effect. It took them a whole second to process information that made no sense. And in that second the nearest of the two guys had taken two 9 mm slugs through the chest. As he went down Sue was shouting, "There are two more coming up the stoop!" And as she shouted she ran. She dove and landed on her belly beside the dead intruder. His colleague about to pull off a shot at Gallin shifted his aim to the running, screaming girl and took a slug to the head from Gallin and another to the heart.

The two guys that charged in had HK 416 assault rifles. The first through the door took four rounds to the chest from Sue and the guy behind him took one to the knee from Gallin. She kicked the door closed and stood on his baby finger.

"You're at a crossroads, pal," she told him. "Walk the rest of your life with a limp, or die here tonight. What's it gonna be?"

He was pale and sweating and obviously in a lot of pain. "Look, lady, it's just a job. I'm no hero."

"Who pays your wages?" He swallowed. He looked very distressed. Gallin smiled. "I guess you are a hero after all."

"No! No, we work for a private security company. Weavers Inc. In Switzerland."

She was still smiling. "Now you know that ain't enough. I am going to give you one more chance."

"Weavers is contracted exclusively to WEFT, World Economic Free Traders, it belongs to Karl Schoff. I can tell you no more than that. It's all I know. We get orders. We obey."

She shot him through the center of his forehead. She looked at Sue who was standing opposite her. "His pals killed Avi. I liked Avi. And they were going to kill two defenseless women. Where did you learn to shoot like that? You been in the army?"

She gave a small shrug. "My dad. I'm from Wyoming, remember?"

"Right. The Cowboy State. So who were these government guys who turned up, and when you say turned up, turned up where?"

"Pinedale. Then they took me to Laramie where this fat guy talked to me."

"Fat guy?"

"Yeah, he was kind of weird. He talked in a weird, old fashioned way."

"I might have known. Nero"

"Yeah, Nero."

"And the other guy was tall, good looking, kind of cool."

"If you like that kind of thing. He said his name was Mason, Alex Mason."

"And you figure Cap might be with them?"

"Maybe, yeah."

"OK, turn off the lights. Let's go. Somebody will come to clean this up." On the way down the steps she said, "You asked if I had called anyone. You think the AI Matrix is monitoring calls."

They climbed into the Range Rover. Sue said, "You know they are. The intelligence services of the major Western allies all have massive listening posts and they all share intelligence. One of the first emergent properties the AI matrix developed was to tap into the listening posts and the exchange networks between the UK the US Canada Australia and New Zealand. Trillions of bits of information swarming across the planet every minute of every day. It stores ninety-nine point nine percent of them. But it can find and select a voice pattern, a name, the voice pattern of a known friend of a person of interest, all and any of that in a nano second." She pointed at the dash. "You want to rip out your GPS. It is watching you right now and knows where you are."

Gallin removed the fuse then fired up the truck and followed Broadway as far as West 42nd Street. There she turned east and drove as far as the massive, gray building that houses the Israeli Consulate on the corner of 42nd and 2nd Avenue. There she turned into a parking garage at the back of the building, where her tires echoed like banshees and her headlamps made shadows leap against the walls. She pulled into a space near an elevator and killed the engine. There she turned to Sue and studied her for a moment.

"You don't know everything," she said eventually. "My guys, my people, we wake up every morning and we go to bed every night facing an existential threat. It's the story of David and Goliath. It doesn't matter whether the threat is invincible. We are all going to die anyway. What is important is how you face your death. You have just two options. Do you go down fighting, or do you commit suicide?" She paused, watching Sue's face. "Some might say the choice is irrelevant if you're going to die anyway. But you know what makes that choice important?" Sue stared at her but didn't answer. Gallin said, "Your soul. Your soul makes it important." She grinned. "Come with me if you want to live."

* * *

A little over two hundred miles away to the south, Karl Schoff sat in General Weisheim's office in the Pentagon and sipped at a glass of the Macallan which he knew had cost only three hundred and fifty dollars a bottle.

"In 2019," he said with a contempt he made no effort to conceal, "a bottle of the Macallan distilled in 1926 sold for a little less than two million dollars." A bland smile creased his flabby cheeks. "I have two dozen of them in my cellar. Of course, I did not pay two million a bottle."

"Once bottled, Karl, it ain't going to mature," the general said, with his ass resting on the edge of the desk. "This tastes just as good."

"But it does not taste as expensive." He sipped again and set the glass down on the occasional table by his side. "What is the situation with Mason and Nero?"

"Mason and Nero are not the problem. The problem is this damned Cap Hohóókee. He is a dangerous man and we don't know for sure where he is. We tracked him to a house in Boulder Flats, near his reservation, but he shot down two of our damned unmarked and escaped into the mountains."

"Surely, Joe, we have the resources to track him and eliminate him."

"Yes," the general nodded elaborately, "if we stop doing other things. AIM already has stunning capabilities. She has linked up to the satellites and the military grids just as your boys predicted, and the emergent properties are off the chart. But she is *thirsty!*"

Schoff spread his hands like he was talking to a cretin. "That's why we need the Caldera!"

The expression on Weisheim's face reflected that on Schoff's. "But *until* we have that power source AIM is all take, take, take. And redirecting satellites and the capabilities of GCHQ and the NSA to look for one man whose greatest skills involve *not* using electronic equipment is a drain on the system."

Schoff sighed. "Always the negative." He laughed. "You remember the song?" He intoned in a ghastly warble, "Eliminate the negative, ac-cent-tchu-ate the positive," he laughed again, "Johnny Mercer. Before my time. Have your men revised Peter Justin's findings?"

"They were fake. Whoever killed him left them there for us to find. The pressure was played down and at the same time the instability was exaggerated. The idea was we would think it was too dangerous to attempt to exploit as an energy source, and if we tried, the carbon nanobots would not be adequate to the pressures in the caldera and would fail. The caldera is stable and will remain stable for centuries yet, and we are taking accurate reading of the internal pressures as we speak."

"How many men have you got there?"

"A dozen. Maybe more. Why?"

Schoff made a distasteful, rotating gesture with his hand. "Are they unwashed scientists with acne, or are they capable men?"

"There are a couple of scientists. The rest are security."

"Fine, fine. Prepare me a helicopter. I will go and supervise. When do the bots arrive?"

"There are a thousand of them at the facility at Bab Tangal. They are still in the process of exposure -"

"Exposure?"

"I thought you were an expert in this stuff?"

"I am an expert at making lots of money. What is exposure and how long will it take?"

"The AI algorithms are subjected to billions of bits of data about which they make decisions. With every mistaken decision they learn and grow smarter. There comes a point when they have learned so much they stop making mistakes. That's exposure."

"When will they be done with exposure?"

"Dr. Amiri tells me they need another twenty-four to forty-eight hours. Then the bots will arrive in a small attaché case through the Pakistan Embassy's diplomatic bag. From DC they will be flown to the cabin."

"Good. Kindly make arrangements, general. I would like to be there by tonight."

FIFTEEN

The sky looked like Odin just told Thor he punched like a girl. It was a heavy sky growing darker by the minute, with low-bellying clouds pregnant with menace and snow. Only the odd, desultory flake wafted in the air, hinting at the cold fury which was in store. The path rose away from us, climbing into the stark hills above the Secret Valley Creek. From where I sat in the saddle on a small quarter horse, following Cap through the wilderness, it looked exposed and vulnerable under that awful sky.

"That looks like snow," I told him. "In September?"

"It looks like unseasonable snow. It never snows in September in these hills. Higher in the mountains, but not here. I can explain to you about how the climate is changing because you made too many factories, but you would say I am preaching."

"How's your leg?"

"It hurts a lot. I try not to think about it."

Eventually the path crested a hill and, as it trailed into deep forest, it petered out and became little more than a long strip of trodden grass. We followed that for half a mile moving toward Blue Mountain. Then we were in among scattered pines that steadily but surely enfolded us, and within fifteen minutes we were in a vast cathedral of green light, following a barely distinguishable path winding through the vast, sighing trees. Birds I could not identify called out from time to time, and their cries had a muted echo under the canopy. Occasionally a wild thrashing of wings erupted overhead, and then settled. We climbed for maybe a mile and a half, with the forested slopes rising ever more steeply either side of us. Then finally we emerged from the trees into rough, wild grassland. The cloud was so low in places it was settling as mist on the mountaintops, and an icy wind was gathering. Cap turned back to me.

"It is just a quarter of a mile now, but we need to move. When you came last time you probably came in a chopper and landed in the meadow. This time we will approach from the back, through woodland. If the fog comes down we can get lost."

The clouds didn't descend into fog, but as we crested the hill the first flakes of snow began to fall. We entered more woodland, not as dense as that lower on the slopes, and when we emerged on the far side I was surprised to see the huge cabin perched high on the crest and maybe a hundred yards in back of it, a series of sheds, barns and smaller cabins set in a rough horseshoe shape around a kind of courtyard, with the open end toward the cabin.

Cap pointed. "That is where we kept all our equipment, and many of the sensors…"

He trailed off because he had seen what I had seen. The ground was slowly turning white under the dusting of flakes. But around the cabin and in between the wooden structures in back of the cabin were four Land

Rovers and two Jeeps. And there were men moving in and out among the buildings.

"Who the hell are these people?"

"You tell me. You are the federal agent."

Even as we spoke we saw one of the Jeeps turn and start speeding up the hill toward us. We came to a halt as they approached. Two men in back and the guy next to the driver climbed out. They all had assault rifles and, though they wee not in uniform, they had military written all over them. The two at the back looked Russian, one had the broad features and powerful back of a Slav. The other was tall and lean. If he'd had hair it would have been blond, and his eyes were pale blue: a Rus, with his roots among the Swedish Vikings.

The guy at the front was a mongrel and when he spoke he had the accent of a South African.

"You can't come here. Who are you? What do you want?"

I moved my horse forward. "I'm going to reach for my ID, sergeant. Don't shoot me."

His weapon shifted and his eyes narrowed. "How'd you know my rank?"

I pulled out my wallet and showed him my card. "Captain Alexander Mason. I'm with the Office of Intelligence at the Pentagon."

He glanced at it, then said, "I asked you a question."

"You're used to giving orders, but I don't see you ever making lieutenant. Now get out of my face and take me to whoever's in charge here. And call me captain."

He jerked his chin at Cap. "What about him... captain?"

"He's with me, and he also made captain in the US

marines. So watch your manners."

We followed them down the long track to the complex of sheds and barns. The wind was picking up and the dense cloud cover was making late afternoon as dark as evening. As we arrived, lights started coming on in the house and in the barns.

We came to a halt in the middle of the horseshoe and the four guys in the Jeep leveled their weapons at us. The big Slav dragged me off my horse and the blond boy wonder dragged Cap down. The air was freezing and my breath billowed as I turned to the Sergeant.

"What the hell is this? I told you who we are."

"Yeah, and it turns out the general has been looking for you all over the Cowboy State. Lucky me. Wait there."

He left toward a cabin that had the appearance of an office. He pushed through the door and while I waited I had a look around. There were two long, low buildings which I guessed were storage for equipment, but the other had the look of a barracks or a dorm. I turned to Cap.

"You had live in workers here?"

His face was impassive, but I could see the rage in his eyes.

"Sometimes, in spring and summer, we brought people from the res' to do drilling, or take the sensors high on the mountains."

I stepped over to the door and pushed it open. Behind me a guard yelled, *"Hey! Don't move!"*

I ignored him and peered through the door. There were a couple of dozen beds on the floor, a small oil burner in the corner, a long table covered in dirty plates. The realization dawned. It was like the icy air had got inside me and clutched my heart in a frozen fist. They were so confident, so sure of what they were doing and what they were going to achieve, they had started already. Protected by their billions, they had recruited labor from the Wind River Reservation, and as soon as they had arrived here they had been subjugated as slaves to start working on the mega-power plant that would feed the AI matrix. They were getting the first taste of what awaited all of us.

The sergeant emerged from the office with a leer on his face. Behind him, in a huge coat, was a man shaped like two pears, with the small one perched on top of the big one. He had loose, pink lips and greedy eyes. He looked over at us and grinned at Cap.

"Hello, how nice to see you again. Good try, but doomed to failure I'm afraid."

He glanced up at the low ceiling of gray cloud. The snow was falling heavier now and already the ground was white. He shifted his gaze to the sergeant.

"Take them away. Break their legs and throw them into the North Pit. I never want to see these sons of bitches again. But Jonah? Make sure it really hurts."

As we were frisked and had our weapons removed I heard him on his cell, saying, "General, your men really need to step up their game. I have just eliminated Alex Mason *and* Cap Hohóókee!"

He shrieked a strangely feminine shriek of laughter and we were shoved toward a Land Rover and bundled in the back. Sergeant Jonah from Seth Efrika and the Slav climbed in to the front seats and in the mirror I saw four guys climb in a Jeep. Then we were roaring back the way we had come. But this time the snow was falling heavily and gusts of wind were whipping them into trailing white ghosts.

We drove for maybe a mile, skidding and slipping down the slope Cap and I had ascended on the horses. Sergeant Jonah said, "We'll need the chains when we go back."

I said, in a wooden voice, "You ain't going back."

It took a second, but they both laughed.

They came off the road and moved through a white field toward a large steel scaffold that housed a drill. They pulled up and the Slave dragged me and Cap out into the snow, which now lay a couple of inches thick on the ground. I saw Cap glance at the Jeep behind us, where grunts were grabbing their weapons and climbing out. There was no urgency because we were not a threat. Sergeant Jonah said, "Over to the well!" Cap took a step toward him, slipped and fell to his knees. The pain on his face was genuine, but when he reached out to me and said, "Mason, help me," that wasn't.

The sergeant took a step toward him, muttering, "What the f -" just as I reached down and grabbed his left wrist and he grabbed mine. Simultaneously, using Cap as support, I slammed my right instep hard into Sergeant Jonah's future generations. After four billion years of evolution, this was the end of his line.

He doubled up wheezing, "Oh, Jesus!"

The second kick, which followed real quick, was to his forehead. That time he didn't call on any prophets. He fell on his face in the snow, and as I bent to pick up his assault rifle, I stamped on the back of his neck for good measure. When you're taking out the trash, you cannot be too thorough.

The guys in the Jeep were still at the 'What the -?' stage, but the Slave had his 416 pointing in my direction and in point two five of a second he was going to tear off my head.

It was instinct. I lifted my feet and pulled the trigger. The force of the bullets erupting from the cannon forced me back as I went down, and I felt the heat of his slugs skim past my face, making the air pop. I was luckier, as I hit the ground four of my rounds tore through his belly and his chest.

There was shouting and bellowing from the Jeep. Cap hurled himself sliding cross the snow toward the hood of the Land Rover, grabbing the Slav's weapon on his way. I rolled and came up on one knee, opening up on the Jeep without aiming, while fountains of snow leapt about me. I had an absolute certainty that within a fraction of a second at least one of those slugs was going to tear into me. There was nothing I could do but roar and scream like something possessed, get to my feet and advance on them emptying the magazine as I went.

I was only vaguely aware of Cap moving at a run around the back of the truck and emptying his weapon on the far side. Between us we fired some seventy rounds at four guys contained within an area of about eighteen square feet, at a distance of maybe fifteen feet. They were probably all dead within the first five seconds, though the assault took fifteen or so. There wasn't a lot left of them, or the Jeep.

Cap approached and looked at them. He said without smiling, "I killed these three."

I arched an eyebrow. "I can tell, mine are all headshots."

"Take the guns. Let's go back and kill the others."

"You're such a fun guy to hang out with, Hohóokee."

He didn't smile. "That's what my flasher pal tells me."

He left me mouthing *"What?"* to myself while I collected the unused rifles and he pulled a plastic bottle of pain killers from his pocket and swallowed a handful of them.

I fitted the chains to the Land Rover and we drove slowly back the way we had come through the deepening snow. The growing cold, the hopelessness of the situation and the impossibility of communicating with Nero, or anybody else for that matter, were all having an insidious effect. A sense of fatalism had invaded my thinking. It was almost suicidal in that I had abandoned any hope of survival, for myself or for humanity. In its place, in the place of hope, there was simply an irresistible drive to kill and destroy as much as I could before I myself was killed and destroyed. Ironically, this fatalism had the collateral effect of removing fear. It occurred to me as I drove down the hill, back toward the complex of buildings, that this was probably the state in which Cap lived permanently. He said to me:

"We are going to die, Mason. You understand that, don't you?"

"I get it. But we do as much damage as we can before we go."

"Our objective is to destroy the drilling holes."

"That's where they plan to introduce the nanobots."

"Yes, and that man in the coat. I have to kill him."

"Who is he?"

"That is Karl Schoff. It might be useless, but if I fail but he dies, it might set the program back a few years."

"Fail?" I said, and glanced at him. "Fail in what, exactly?"

He didn't answer straight away. We stopped in the

horseshoe. There were a couple of guys overseeing a bunch of Indians loading bits of a drill into the back of a truck. They took no notice of us. We swung down from the Land Rover and stood looking around. I guess neither of us was exactly sure what to do next.

That was when the tall Russian with the pale blue eyes came out of the office scowling at us.

"What you are doing? Where is Zelco?"

I said, "The Jeep broke down. He told us to come and get the jack."

"Go stand by wall, over there!"

I smiled at him, "Have you got a knife?"

He scowled at me, then called to one of his men. "Rich! Come here! These guys comin' back." Rich, a big hulking guy with long hair and a beard, who'd been supervising the loading of the drill growled at the Indians, "Take it out to well sixteen. You, Ben, go inside and get your dinner. I'll be in in five." He ambled over as Ben made his way toward the house. The Russian said to us, "Go stand by wall! Stupid question..."

I shrugged. "Just grant a condemned man a wish. I'm not asking to marry your sister. I'm just asking you if you have a knife!"

"No! I don't got a knife! OK? Now go stand by the goddamn wall!"

I looked at Rich. "What about you, Rich? You've got that outdoor look, huntin' shootin' fishin'. Have you got a knife?"

He observed me with hooded eyes. "Where's Pete and the boys? What in hell are you doin' here?"

I felt a deadly emotion inside, that was at the same time a complete absence of emotion. It was a certainty of death, mine or another's. It made no difference. "All I am asking, Rich, is a simple question. I don't know why you're having trouble answering it. I've told you, the Sergeant told us to come and get a jack. Now, what *I* am asking *you* is, have you got a knife?"

He was having trouble computing. He could not process what was going down, and he was getting mad. He creased his eyes and shook his head and pointed at the wall. "Yeah, I got a knife and if you don't get over by the damned wall I'm going to use it to spill your guts. Move!"

I smiled. "That's good news, Rich."

"What the hell are you -?"

"All our guns are in the Land Rover, but if you have a knife, I can use that to kill you with."

SIXTEEN

Two seconds of incomprehension is all you need. I lunged a long step forward like I was fencing and smashed my fist into his sternum at the end of a rigid arm. A blow like that is so painful it can cause cardiac arrest. Every breath is like drawing needles into your lungs.

It took me less than a second to reach under his jacket and find the large, broad-bladed hunting knife. Pete was gaping, but by the time he'd put his rifle to his shoulder it was too late. I had stepped behind him and driven the razor sharp blade deep into the side of his neck. Then I punched forward, partly decapitating him. He fell rigid on his face and spilled his red lifeblood all over the white snow.

I went back to Rich. He was turning blue and making painful noises in his throat. I can be as ruthless as the next guy when I have to be, but I don't believe in cruelty, or causing unnecessary suffering. So I turned his head to expose the left side of his neck and drove the blade deep through his jugular and his carotid. Life moved out and death moved in, in a couple of heartbeats.

Cap was standing immobile, exactly where he had

been. He was watching me. "You are a very dangerous man, Alex Mason."

"That's what my driving instructor kept telling me."

He sighed and turned to the Indians who were standing at the truck watching us.

"Where are the men who are supervising you?"

A young boy, no more than sixteen, answered. "They gone for dinner. We still got a lot of work to do before we can eat. If we don't do the work, they beat us."

"How many people has he brought here from the Res?"

"Maybe a hundred. They beat us. They promised us good money and good conditions for work, but they beat us and whip us, and there are rumors they killed a couple of guys who gave them trouble."

"You need to go. Go to the men who are digging the wells." He went to our Land Rover and pulled out the weapons we had there. "Kill the guards and tell your people to get away. Go as far as you can. The mountain is going to blow. Go."

They clambered in the trucks and the Jeeps and fled, driving fast, skidding in the snow. They left only the truck with the drill.

"That's good," I said. "You gave them all our weapons and our vehicles."

He kept his eyes on the receding trucks and said quietly, "You don't need weapons, and you don't need a vehicle."

"Man, you really are like that, aren't you. It's not an act. So now what?"

He smiled. "Now we go inside and kill everybody. By the looks of it, you are good at that. It must be genetic."

"I just told you. You gave away our weapons."

He looked past me toward the house, a hundred yards away. "No time to talk now." I followed his gaze. There was a guy outside the door. He was down on one knee with a rifle at his shoulder. Cap said, "Do my work. Go to well nine. It is close. You'll know what to do there. Good bye, Alex Mason."

There was a puff of smoke from the rifle. A fraction of a second later came the crack and Cap whiplashed as a fountain of red blood ejected from the back of his head. He fell straight back and for a moment I felt like everything drained out of me, leaving behind only a black void of hopelessness.

I was vaguely aware that the guy was now aiming at me. I took a step to my right, behind the truck and felt the hard, sharp smack of a slug hitting the drilling equipment beside me. Instinctively I yelled like I'd been hit, and began to whimper loudly as I took hold of a sledge hammer that lay in the back of the truck among the pieces of the drill. I heard the running trudge of feet and kept whimpering. He skidded round the back of the truck and I leered at him. "Surprise!"

I brought the hammer up hard under his chin. He staggered and his eyes rolled and I brought it down in a vicious swing onto his skull, which caved in under the savagery of the blow.

I am not given to rages, but when I'd seen Cap di, falling back into the white snow, something had snapped inside. A rage was building in me that I had no power to control. It was a rage at the needless killing of a good man, because he did not fit the program, a rage against the bloated, greedy parasites who destroy lives, destroy people, destroy hope and happiness and humanity just so they can suck another ounce of privilege from the world. It was a wild, untamable rage against the stupidity and greed of those who build marble temples to themselves while they crush humanity under their heel, drink their blood and sentence them to death or slavery.

I began to walk, holding the hammer in my hand. I could have taken the guy's rifle and sidearm, but I wanted to get close and personal. They had sentenced me to death, and while they sat gorging, they assumed I was lying, bleeding, with broken legs, in a well in the snow. But I was not dead, nor was the human race that stood behind me, and while there was breath in my lungs and blood in my veins, I would unleash my rage on these bastards.

I kicked in the door and walked into the kitchen. I could make out a long table across the huge living area, and a large fire burning in the fireplace. I could hear laughter, the clinking of glasses and bottles, voices raised in noisy conversation. Karl Schoff's voice reached me: "Is the bastard dead yet? He's as hard to kill as a bionic rat!"

There was laughter.

I stepped through the broad arch into the living area. They had a table down the center of the room. Schoff was at the head with his back to me. At a glance I took in seven men either side and one at the far end. Sixteen men total.

The table was laden with food, roasted meats, vegetables, dishes full of potatoes, and eight bottles of wine which stood in a line down the center. There were also bottles and jugs of beer scattered here and there. It was maybe four paces away. I stood watching them, feeling the rage of hatred building to an eruption inside me. Silence settled on the room. They all stared at me.

I heard Schoff say, "What?" staring at them from one to another. I snarled, "Yes, he's dead."

I ran three steps. I knew I was going to die, but I didn't care. Death comes to us all sooner or later, and this was as good a way to die as I could think of. Schoff's flabby face was turning in slow motion. I slammed the handle of the hammer into his head and he sprawled, gaping across his food, sending wine and roast meat crashing and flying. Then I leapt.

I leapt high, raising the hammer over my head, and, as my feet touched the table top, I swung it down first left where it caved in a man's face as he gaped and screamed, and then right into the head of a man who was scrambling to his feet. I was aware I was bellowing and snarling, as though I was possessed by some monstrous being. All about me I could see screaming, shouting faces. I kicked one and saw blood and teeth explode from his mouth. I smashed the hammer into another and saw him fall back, jerking and quivering. In front of me a couple of guys were scrambling onto the table. Three of them had guns in their hands and were waving them in my direct. I heard the smack of a shot and plowed the hammer through them twice, describing a savage X. I saw arms horribly broken and twisted, I saw wild eyes and screaming mouths, I saw necks break and blood gushing everywhere, mixing with the spilled wine and the broken glass.

I heard more shots but I was oblivious to them. I jumped down from the table and smashed the iron head of the hammer into a back I saw there. I felt the ribs and the vertebrae crush, but I was already moving on in an insane frenzy, crashing the hammer down on a shoulder, feeling the bones break and the muscles tear.

And then they were running, scrambling, falling over each other , some through the front door, others out the back. I stood staring all about me. It was a massacre, an orgy of gore and murder. There were bodies lying across the table, bodies, broken and twisted lying on the floor. I could hear a voice moaning, whimpering. I found the owner and as I looked down at him his eyes glazed and he died. I counted the bodies. Seven.

Out, through the big windows I could see a green chopper landing. Men were running, scattering this way and that. I went to Karl Schoff. His face was badly bruised, but his eyes were open and he was groaning.

"You don't look much like a demigod, Karl."

He looked up at me and began to sob. "You're insane."

"That's kind of rich coming from you, Karl. You dream of godliness while you sentence humanity to extinction."

"It's for the good of the planet. There are too many of you, and so ignorant and primitive."

"But you get to live, enhanced by AI,"

He nodded, a trembling nod, "And it enhanced by us."

I laughed. It was an ugly, manic laugh. "You? You are going to enhance AI? How?"

"With feelings. Those who survive, the best of the race, free from sexual separation or prejudice, free from mental limitations or restrictions, we will allow the matrix to tap in to our emotions and become one with us, sentient," he nodded, "You said the word, godly."

"And I am insane. With your obscene power and riches you have brought humanity to the brink of extinction, but I am insane. You believe that you can attain godliness, but I – me - I am insane."

I heard the voice behind me and recognized it. It was Weisheim. He said, "Sweet mother of god! What the hell happened here?"

I put the hammer on my shoulder and stood behind Schoff. "Humanity kicked back," I said. Half a dozen men in uniform filed in behind him. He took a moment to gaze at the table and the scattered bodies.

"These people you've killed. They don't signify. They are nobody. You have achieved nothing."

"What about this slob here? Does he signify? Is he anybody? Would it set you back a lot if I crushed his skull?"

"You'd be dead before the blow fell."

"You want to bet? Shall we give it a try?"

He held out a hand. "Now just take it easy, son."

"I am not your son, general. I am a federal officer of the United States, and I am placing you under arrest for treason."

He chuckled. He looked back at the soldiers behind him. "You have to admire a guy like this. If you hadn't caused so much damage – what is it two choppers, I don't know how many men -"

I cut across him. "I'm not finished yet, general. I'm going to kill you and I am going to take this piece of crap back to Washington with me so he can explain to Congress just how crazy you have become in your military-industrial national security clique."

The patronizing smile faded from his face. It was replaced by an expression of dangerous contempt. "No," he said. "You won't do any of that. Because as I said, you will be dead. He turned to the man on his right and said, "Kill him."

The guy didn't hesitate. He put his rifle to his shoulder and took aim. For a fraction of a second, beyond him, I saw another chopper. It made no sense to me and in a resurgence of my rage I brought the hammer crashing down on Schoff's head and hurled myself across the floor amid a hail of bullets.

My madness had gone to another level. I had understood during our journey to the cabin what Pete, Cap and Sue had planned. I scrambled to my feet and ran up the stairs to the den with splinters of wood flying around my feet and bullets raked the staircase. I ignored them because I had an image in my mind that was driving me.

I stumbled into the vast area of the upper floor and saw again the map of the area hanging on the wall. This time I paid attention. I could hear boots running on the stairs behind me. I ignored them. The map filled my vision and my mind. I saw the bright yellow pins and then I saw that well number nine, a mile to the north of the cabin, had a red pin, not a yellow one.

I arrived at the head of the stairs just a guy in fatigues, with pale blue eyes and freckles arrived. He saw me a second after I saw him. That second was all I needed to grab the barrel of his HK416 in my right had and smash my right instep between his legs. His gape was as much disbelief as it was pain. I wrenched the rifle from his hands, spun it and shoved the muzzle against his belly. There were two guys in uniform behind him, half way up the stairs. They were shouting at me to cease and desist, aiming their rifles at me but unwilling to shoot their pal. I grinned at him.

"Why," I said, "When I am having so much fun?"

I double tapped and as he fell back I took out the two soldiers behind him. Then I was running down the stairs, in the certain knowledge that I would be dead by the time I reached the door; but in the absolute knowledge also that I would go down killing. I would not stop until I had either reached well nine, or I was dead.

But when I reached the ground floor the place was empty but for the corpses scattered around the long table. I advanced to the kitchen with the rifle at my shoulder but found no one. So I returned at a run to the table, snatched a couple of side arms which I shoved in my belt.

A glance through the window showed me an unmarked chopper hovering maybe a hundred yards away, kicking up dense clouds of snow. I made a mental note, then ran.

SEVENTEEN

I ran out into the snow. It was falling heavier and visibility was down to maybe fifty yards. The chances of getting lost in this white world were high. But I had noted on the map that well number nine was a mile north along the ridge upon which the cab had been built. Whether this was coincidental or deliberate I had no idea, but I did know that if I didn't go down any steep hills, or climb any steep slopes, I would come to the well shaft in about an hour's time.

I began to walk fast. The snow was three or four inches deep, enough to cover my boots, but I knew that within twenty minutes or half an hour I would be wading. Combined with the plunging temperatures and my exhaustion, the chances of making it to the well were slim.

The chances of making it back did not exist. This was the end of the road. This was where the story ended. Game over.

I passed the truck with the hardware for the well in the back. I wrenched open the door in the forlorn hope that I might find the keys in the cab. They weren't there and I knew that in that biting, penetrating cold there was no way my fingers would let me jump start it. So I slammed the door again and set off at a slow jog. If I could make up as much distance as possible before I had to start wading, I stood a fractionally better chance.

But it didn't take long for the wading to start. The snow was coming in from the east and it was drifting in large pockets along the irregular ridge where it rose in a slight incline toward the hills. My feet had grown numb in my boots and I had that odd mixture of pain and insensibility in my toes that tells you you are headed for frostbite. My clothes, jeans, leather hiking boots and a jacket, were totally unsuited to the snow. But the snowstorm had been unseasonable and unexpected. And above all time had been against us, as it was now.

Behind me I could hear the irregular crackle of automatic fire. It made me wonder. My brain was slowing and the intense cold was biting through my skin, freezing my blood and biting into my lungs as I breathed. It was hard to follow a clear train of thought. But I was aware that the gunfire was far off, and thre were no rounds kicking up the snow around me. So that meant that the shots were not directed at me.

At who then? An image of Nero rose up in my mind, with his deep, brown eyes and his aquiline nose. "I believe, Alex, you mean at *whom!*"

That made me laugh. "May as well die cheerful," I told myself, and heard my voice shaking and my jaw juddering. I focused on my feet and concentrated on setting a steady rhythm. I told myself that would keep the blood flowing. I felt drunk and tried to speak aloud, "All of the disadvantages and none of the pleasure," but my lips were freezing, and the attempt to articulate the 'A' sound was like sanpaper in my throat.

I walked, trudged, tried to run a few steps. I fantasized about ripping off a sleeve and wrapping it around my mouth and nose to stop them from freezing. But I knew that if I stopped I would slip into hypothermia. I had to die – I knew I had to die – but I had to die having done what I had come to do.

Nero wagged a fat finger at me. "Do not die in the attempt! Die in the doing!"

The big log fire behind him made him warm and I could feel my feet and my hands thawing in the red and amber glow.

The jolt as my face hit the snow woke me up and I struggle to my feet, wondering in a sleepy panic how long I had been lying there.

"There is no try," Nero told me as I waded on. I noticed he had pointed green ears and it suddenly made perfect sense that he was Yoda disguised as a human genius. It explained everything about him. The food on Dagobah was probably awful, and that was why he loved Earth food so much.

That got me to wondering if Lovelock was from another planet too. It would explain her extreme beauty and how she could be married to a freak like Nero. As he handed me the glass of Napoleon Brandy I laughed and told him, "Come on, come clean. You *are* Yoda, aren't you?"

"My dear boy, it has taken you long enough to work it out."

"And you *are* married to Lovelock, aren't you?"

"Lovelock is a life saver," he said, rather ambiguously. "We all have to save lives from time to time. And she is a life saver."

My eyes opened. I wondered if I was lying down. I could feel nothing but a numb pain that seemed to define all of me. Sluggishly I worked out I was standing up by the angle of the trees around me. The need to sleep was a desperation located around my eyes and in my lungs. The rest of me was already asleep.

Ahead of me, maybe twenty or thirty feet away I could see a giant, black ghost; a black shroud glimpsed through the drifting flakes. He was immensely tall and thin, and brought a message of death.

I dragged my right foot forward, then my left. I felt I was freezing where I stood. Five more agonizing steps brought me to within six or seven feet of the ghosts giant, iron leg. He rose out of a large hole in the ground where the snow was drifting in. This told me he was a Shade from the underworld. And I knew his name.

"Magma!" I shouted it and felt no pain because I was shouting with my mind. "Magma! I know why you are here. You are here because tonight all of humanity will die. You are here to gather up the souls of the dead and take them down into the bowels of the Earth. We have not been good custodians. We have betrayed you and abused you, and now we must die. I know that. We must die before they steel your power for the heartless mind of the AI. I know this."

I took another step closer, aware I was in a frozen fantasy, but not sure how to get out, or where reality lay.

"Show me," I said. "Show me what Cap and Pete and Sue installed here. Show me what to do."

Another step took me to the edge of the shaft. It was a good ten feet across with an iron railing running around it. A brief, passing moment of clarity showed me that the great, black daemon was the framework of the drill, and over on my left there was a red box, three or four foot long, three feet high and a couple of feet deep. Iaw it was padlocked and staggered a couple of steps till I was close enough to shoot off the padlock. It was hard and I had the feeling my fingers would snap off when I pulled the trigger.

The shot echoed, a high whine among the grayness and among the pines. I got down on my knees and opened the box. There were dials and digital displays. There were wires, lots of them that disappeared into heavy casings for cables. I struggled to focus my mind to make sense of what I was seeing, but my thinking was sluggish and slow. I tried to put the pieces together in my mind. There were bulbs, red bulbs that were not illuminated. Each had a number: four, five, eighteen. And above number nine there was a button, a red button that said release.

My hand seemed to move of its own volition. I reached out and my numb fingers hovered over the button.

And then there was a noise. It was like a gnat, or a mosquito, buzzing in my ear. I wondered if I was about to pass out, or die. I had to press the button. The buzzing got louder. I fought to reach across the remaining three inches, which were like a vast abyss in my mind, but some force I did not understand held my arm.

Then Cap was there. He sat next to where I was kneeling, trembling in the cold.

"I am freezing," I told him. "I am dying of cold." He didn't seem to be cold. He was just calmly watching me.

"The button," he said. "Number nine. Press it."

"Why? I don't think I can."

"If the AI matrix gets this power, humanity will be exterminated, Mason. Do you understand that." I was going to answer but he went on. "I am not talking about Mankind, I am talking about humanity. The spirit that gives us a soul, that gives us compassion and makes out hearts burn with life."

"And this button...?"

"Is our last resort. It's the fall back from our fall back. You will release high explosive charges at key points along a fault line. Pete calculated the explosives would be enough to weaken the fault enough to provoke an eruption. That data never went to Schoff or to Washington."

"And when I press it, it could provoke -"

"It will provoke an extinction event."

My hand was still trembling over the button. "So what's the difference between this and the AI matrix?"

"Press that button and Mankind and his humanity, might survive. Even if it is in small, struggling tribes. But he will stand a chance. Do not press it, and humanity will be lost forever, consumed into the matrix, consumed into the great Hive."

I wept and the tears froze to my cheeks.

The voice I heard next was not Cap's. It was a shrill scream behind me: *Do it! Do it! For Christ's sake do it!*"

And another voice yelling, "*Stop! Stop or I'll shoot!*"

They were simultaneous. In a fraction of a second I realized I was suffering the hallucinatory madness before death by by hypothermia, and in that same fraction of a second the pure logic of Cap's reasoning gave me light and a purpose before death. I reached forward and my numb, frozen fingers touched the button.

The blow was like being struck by a speeding truck. It hurled me sprawling in the freezing snow with agonizing shjafts of pain stabbing through every part of my body. A black form rose above me, stting astride my and yelled at me, *"Don't move!"*

Then it was gone and I was struggling to get back on my feet. My dazed mind was telling me that spirits and daemons were beginning to emerge from the well. I tried to say we were at End of Days, but I could not move my mouth. As I rose on one knee I saw a woman in a thick, quilted blue jacket kneeling where I had knelt moment before. It made no sense but she too was reaching in to press the button.

I tried to say, "Be careful of the daemon," but only managed to grunt a noise. Then the black form was on her in a whirl of violence, dragging her away. And that was when I saw her face.

Sue.

My brain groaned. Sue was on her feet, struggling furiously with the creature in black, screaming at her. She clawed at her head and face and the daemon's hood came away. I reeled.

"Gallin?" I croaked. *"Gallin?"*

It happened ina couple of seconds, no more, but I saw it in slow motion. Gallin's feet slipped on a stone concealed by the snow. Her feet went from under her and she fell at the edge of the well. I watched as Sue kicked at her and pushed her over the edge. She rolled, slipped and vanished from view. Except that her hands clamped onto the iron railing.

I ran, stumbling and in agony, emitting a horrible cry from my frozen throat and mouth. As I did so, Sue was scrambling on all fours to the open box. I reached over the railing and grabbed Gallin's wrist. She stared into my face and screamed *"Stop her!"*

I looked and saw Sue rise up on her knees. In my frozen, stupefied brain some neuron sparked and made me realize that if Sue pressed the button Gallin would die incinerated. And that changed everything. I reached behind my back, pulled one of the pistols I had taken from the cabin and fired instinctively. She was barely six feet away, and the shot was intended to strike her arm. But my fingers were frozen and insensible, and my whole body was trembling with the cold. The bullet hit the box and ricocheted into her shoulder. She screamed, half stood, staggered back and fell in the snow.

I reached down and dragged her from the well. As she stepped over the rail I tried to say, "What the hell are you doing here?" but got only as far as "Wha," which was all I could say. But in any case she had enveloped me in her arms and held me close and tight, and I felt the warmth of her body infuse mine.

Then I felt the hand gun slip out of my waistband. I heard Gallin's voice shout, "*Stop!*" and a second later the explosive crack of the gun. I turned to look. Sue was lying sprawled over the box. Her hood was back and her blond hair was bright red. By degrees she slipped and tumbled into the deep well.

Gallin went and closed the box. Then she came to me, pulling off her jacket and wrapped it around me.

"What the hell were you doing, Mason? Come on, I have a snow mobile here. We need to get you heated up from the inside, you crazy son of a bitch. Another couple of minutes and you'd be dead."

She fired the engine and we pulled away, buzzing through the heavy sheets of thick-falling snow under a low gray ceiling. It was only a mile, but a mile in the snow in Wyoming can be the longest road you will ever walk, and it will not necessarily lead you home. It might lead you, as I had learned, to the doors of hell.

As we approached the horseshoe of barns at the back of the cabin. I saw troops in uniform patrolling with assault rifles. I tapped Gallin's shoulder and pointed. She leaned back and I saw her cheeks were flushed with the cold and when she spoke her voice was trembling.

"Marines," she said, "Under General McAffee. They'll keep it real."

After that I don't remember much.

EIGHTEEN

Some seven thousand miles away, at the secret facilities in the mountains of Bab Tangal, just north of Zarand, the skies were a perfect blue under the dome of heaven. There was a stillness and a silence under the molten sun, that had even the flies immobilized and listless.

The scream came out of the empty sky, small at first, like a sharp, silver needle, then growing louder, building towards a horrific crescendo. But sound is much slower than light, and by the time the people of Zarand had heard the demoniacal scream coming out of the empty sky, the three B2 Spirits were already fanning out and heading back to base in Israel, and the salvo of deep penetration missiles had torn a deep hole in the side of the mountain.

The attack was never reported on the news, and if it had been Israel would have denied it vehemently, not least because Israel does not have B2 Spirit stealth bombers. What happened next however was reported, in a slightly altered manner.

The single Cruise missile streaked through the sky and straight into the cavity opened up by the deep penetration missiles. The tactical nuclear explosion that followed was largely contained by the mountain, but penetrated deep into the warren of vast corridors and chambers that housed the Bab Tangal nano-particle research facility, shattering the structure, caving in the chambers, passages and living quarters, disintegrating the computer networks, vaporizing all the data contained there and, most important of all, it vaporized the nanocarbon bots which were in their final stages of exposure.

What was reported on the news was that an Iranian secret nuclear missile silo had exploded, causing Israel, the United States and the United Kingdom to demand, at the United Nations, immediate access to Iranian research.

I was informed of all this by Gallin while I lay in bed and slowly recovered from frostbite and hypothermia at my hotel in Jackson. When she had finished I croaked, "But we are not done. We may have treated a couple of the symptoms, but the infection is still there, and it runs deep."

"You're not wrong, Mason," she said. "A *really* big problem has come out of left field. The nerds and the geeks have been warning about this for over forty years, but nobody really believed it could happen." She got off the bed and went to gaze out of the window at the terrace. "It's like Frankenstein's monster," she said to the glass, "only in that case it was Frankenstein, the scientist, who wanted to bring the monster to life. But now, in this case, it's the scientists themselves who want to shut him down, and it's the politicos and the billionaires who want to give it life."

She turned from the window and rested her ass on the sill to watch me for a moment in silence.

"This is going to cause a lot of conflict," she said. "I mean internal conflict, between departments, governors and senators, individual states and branches of the federal government. Hell, within the federal government itself."

"It promises power beyond anything we can imagine, but it will never deliver."

"There are a lot of people in DC," she said, "who see this as the next stage in evolution and an opportunity to become mega powerful. We are talking both sides of the house in the White House and on the Hill. Those people are back and in many cases paid by the billionaires' club."

"What's the feeling in Israel about this?"

"I was just going to say, aside from a few crazy billionaires, the feeling in Israel and the UK, is that this is a loose cannon that needs to be secured."

The bell sounded and she left the room to go and open the suite door. There were voices and a moment later a waiter cam in with a trolley laden with food, wine and champagne set about a silver soup tureen. Behind the waiter were Gallin and Nero.

"The soup is chicken soup, richly peppered and laced with olive oil," he said. 'It has great curative qualities." He handed the waiter twenty bucks and said, "You may leave. The lady will dispense the food."

The waiter bowed and left, Gallin began spooning chicken soup into a deep bowl and Nero beetled his brows at me.

"How are you?"

"I'm fine," I croaked. "Why?"

He arched one of the brows he had been beetling and said, "Unwarranted, Alex. What were you doing at the well?"

"I don't remember," I lied. "I guess I was trying to disable the trigger mechanism. Cap had asked me to detonate the explosives." He grunted lifted the lid on a dish and started spooning raw, live oysters onto a plate. I added, "I hallucinated that you were Yoda and you were married to Lovelock."

I glanced at Gallin. She hid her smiled and we both studied Nero's face. "And what," he asked as he poured himself a glass of Manzanilla, makes you think that was an hallucination?"

He sat and there might have been a trace of a smile on his face.

"General Weisheim has stated categorically that he went there to arrest Schoff and stop the abuse of the Wind River reservation by Schoff's men. Naturally his men back him up and corroborate his story. He also claims that you murdered somewhere in the region of a dozen men or more, and tried to kill him."

"Can you silence him?" I asked.

"Yes, you and Captain Gallin will have to entrap him by recording a confession. If that fails you will have to assassinate him." He sucked an oyster from its shell and swallowed it, then sipped some wine. "Naturally," he said, setting down his glass, "ODIN will disavow you if you are caught, because we do not exist."

Gallin and I blinked at each other a moment, then I croaked, "Is he in DC?"

"He is at his Ranch outside Pinedale. You are booked on a flight tomorrow morning to DC. The flight will be taken by a couple similar to yourselves. You, in the meantime, will penetrate the ranch, recover any data he might have relating to the Caldera project, deal with him and, if necessary, burn down the house." He gave me a long, level look. "I hope I have made myself very clear, Alex."

"Very," I said, "and I have to say I am touched by your faith in me. Most people might think that in the condition I am in I might need some rest. But not you, sir. You know I can take it."

He sucked another oyster and regarded me while he swallowed and sipped.

"If you don't feel up to it, Alex, I can always send somebody else."

"No, sir. I'll be there. Don't you worry."

"Sir," it was Gallin. Her cheeks were flushed and her eyes were bright. "I am overstepping the line, but you must see that Mason is in no condition -"

"Captain Gallin, what I must or must not see is entirely my affair. What I do see is that General Weisheim is an extremely dangerous man who underpins an extremely dangerous association that is an existential threat to the United States and the wider world." He stood. "We, like you in the Mossad, do not sign up to be massaged and mollycoddled, captain. We sign up in the full knowledge that we expose ourselves to the three Ds – Danger, Damage and Death."

He walked to the door. There he stopped and looked back at us. To Gallin he said, "It is not easy to take the decision to expose a valued operative and a friend to mortal danger. You know that from your personal experience. But Alex did not elect to be a hairdresser. He elected to work for me. And I must be coherent in my decisions."

To me he said. "I wish you a speedy recovery. Drink the soup."

And he left.

We heard the suite door close and Gallin shook her head. "Asshole!"

I sighed. "He's right, though."

"You are in no condition." She sat on the bed and held my hand. "You're a tough Son of a bitch, Mason. But right now you're weak. If we encounter resistance at that place, you don't stand a chance." She gave a small laugh. "A half crippled tough guy with hypothermia and severe frostbite, and a female intelligence officer whose most challenging encounters involve stopping her superior officers from touching her ass."

I frowned at her and drew breath, but she leaned forward and kissed me softly on the mouth. Her right hand slipped under the sheet and she touched my bare side. When she pulled back she was looking me straight in the eye. "Don't speak. Try to get some rest. I have to go out for a few hours, but I'll be back to see how you are."

I slid down in the bed. She switched off the light and I lay staring at the ceiling and wondering how the hell I was now supposed to sleep. She left the bedroom door ajar and after a moment I heard the suite door close.

Half an hour later I was still staring at the ceiling. A very small part of my brain was wondering how the hell I was going to carry out my orders for the next day, the other ninety-nine percent of it was wondering what the hell had just happened and how this was going to impact on the rest of my life – however short that 'rest' might be.

I heard the suite door open and close and felt a hot shot of adrenalin burn in my belly. When she came in I was going to have to ask her why she had – and what – and I couldn't bring myself to say it.

I heard her moving about the suite, told myself

what the hell! And sat up. Then the door to the bedroom opened and there were three guys silhouetted in it. They were big, over six foot and built like draft horses. A fourth man appeared behind them and as they moved into the room and took up positions around the bed he flipped on the switch. I said:

"Weisheim,"

He wasn't smiling. "So you're going to come to my ranch, my home, invade my property, torture and interrogate me, and then you are going to kill me and burn down my house."

"You bugged my room," I said half to myself.

"How do you think I am feeling right now, Mason?"

"Warm and fuzzy?"

"Always the wiseass. You know what I am going to do, Mason?"

"Engage in a meaningful dialogue and talk me to death?"

"I am going to sit here and watch while my boys beat you half to death. At some point you little Jew girl will show up and we'll invite her in for a party. We'll rape her and beat her half to death and then we'll take you both up to Green River Lake and leave you there to die. You'll be praying the exposure gets you before the bears do, believe me."

"Well, gee! I'm just so flattered you thought of us."

He sighed softly and gave his head a hopeless little shake.

"You know what I am going to enjoy most? Knowing that your last, dying thoughts will be that all you managed to do, you smug little asshole, was to delay things. It would have been better for you to blow the

Caldera. That would have stopped us and you would have stood a minimal chance of survival, to start over. But now? You will never stop us The best of us will evolve, and the rest of you will die. Take him and beat him, but don't kill him."

They advanced on me two on my left and one on my right. Under the sheet I had already taken hold of the Sig Gallin had slipped me when she gave me the kiss. I shifted it and blew a couple of holes in the nearest guy on my left. I heard the general cry out in pain. The goon on my right turn and ran for the door. Gallin was there to meet him. Her first kick went to his knee. He keened in pain and her second kick went between his legs. He collapsed and she lunged toward the third guy who was rushing her. She blocked his swinging right hook with her left and simultaneously rammed a straight right to the tip of his jaw. He went down like a felled tree.

I was up by then. I shot him in the head and she went back and broke the castrato's neck. That left General Weisheim, who was standing with his back against the wall and What-the-Hell all over his face. Gallin gave her head a little twitch.

"We knew you'd bugged the room, Weisheim. So we let you know how weak Mason was, and me? Well I'm just a defenseless little Jew girl you can rape and murder at will. And just so you know, Mr Evolution, right now there are a hundred marines swarming over your house, directed by Nero. And when they're done you house will evolve into smoke and ashes."

"You can't do this to me," he blustered. "Do you know how much weight I carry in DC?"

"Your house will evolve into ashes," I told him, "your demi-god friends in DC will evolve into has-beens, and you will die."

And I shot him without hesitation, right between the eyes.

EPILOGUE

The bodies had been cleared. The management of the hotel were being 'spoken to', in Nero's words, as was the Teton Sheriff's Department. Meanwhile down in Sublette County the national media were being alerted to the fire which had broken out in General Weisheim's ranch outside Pinedale. It was not clear yet whether the general had been in residence or not, but some believed he had been, and it would not be long before his charred remains were found.

"I have informed the manager he must arrange another suite for you. I recommend you remain here a few days to recover, then take a month's holiday."

I smiled and shrugged. "You know me, sir, obedience is my middle name."

He didn't laugh or smile. He stood. I said, "Sir, can we beat this? All we've done is delay it, give ourselves breathing space at most."

"We are at war, Alex. The enemy has surprised us on our left flank. We have fought him off, but we are now at war." He paused. "To answer your question, we must eliminate those who would open the gates of Troy to the wooden horse. Because, if ever that horse gets in –

if ever AI achieves a great enough energy source to take complete control – we will be annihilated." He took a deep breath. "There are people who were at that meeting, Alex, who need to be eliminated. But that is not our job. I have spoken to the brigadier, and Cobra will take care of it."

"Cobra?"

"I'll explain at some other time. But know that it is in hand."

He left and Gallin and I sat looking at each other. She was on the bed in the half-lotus position. I was in a chair, dressed but feeling like I should be in bed. She said:

"So Cap and Sue had decided that, if they could not convince Schoff and his associates in Washington that the Caldera was not viable, they would have to provoke an eruption that would either drive humanity to extinction, or to the brink of extinction and shut down AI permanently. A reset on steroids."

I nodded. Sue and Cap had decided that Pete wouldn't have the strength to do it. So when the final data came in showing that the Caldera was stable, either sue or Cap – I believe it was Sue – waited for him at the cabin, and they shot him."

She frowned. "What I don't get is why they didn't set off the charges right then."

I raised my shoulders. "We'll probably never know, but my guess is that the explosives in the wells were a last resort fall back solution. There was no guarantee that it would work. Plan A was the one Sue had cultivated in New York, where she had made contact with Sam Goldman, a noted opponent of AI. When she told him that they wanted to find somebody in Russia or Iran to sell them a Tactical Nuclear Device, he contacted Mossad, and you set up your trap."

She nodded. "That makes sense. And when she and Cap lost contact with each other, he went for the fallback position. Meanwhile Schoff and his coconspirators in DC had moved in for the kill." She frowned again. "Why did they call you in? That seems stupid."

"It was, kind of. They wanted to know who killed Pete and why. If it was Cap or Sue maneuvering for a bigger share of the profits, that was fine. But if it wasn't, it could be a problem waiting to happen. They thought they could set us to investigate and control us while we did it. And that was a mistake. On the other hand, Nero believes there are people in the administration and in Congress who are worried about AI, and they wanted ODIN involved because Nero has a reputation for integrity as well as smarts."

We sat in silence for a moment. "Strange times," she said at last.

"And speaking of which," I said, with a smile and an odd burn in my belly, "Why did you kiss me?"

She raised her eyebrows. "Well I *am* sorry! I do apologize! Was it that awful?"

"Not in the least!" I said hastily. 'I enjoyed it. But it was a surprise."

"Well keep your pajamas on your own washing line, kiddo. Nero and I knew the place was bugged, but we didn't know if they had cameras. We had decided to put on a show that we intended to hit them, but that you were really weak and I was just a desk clerk, in the hope it would draw them here before we went there. That was Weisheim's style, after all."

"Oh," I said. "Well, that would explain it. Only," I frowned at her again. "Couldn't you have kissed me on the forehead, or the top of my head, or my cheek…"

"Yes," she said, "but I had just said I was an intelligence officer who never saw any action and, Mason? I needed to shut you up. Not for the first time or, I am sure, or for the last."

I gave a single, slow nod. "So, you never see any action as an intelligence officer, and you were hoping to see some action?"

"The state you're in? In your dreams, pal!"

"What, you think I can't take you right now?"

"Take me? You? Ha!"

Fortunately, or not, the manager appeared at that moment to say they had arranged another suite, and Gallin helped me, with surprising tenderness, to hobble to the door.

Be the first to receive Alex Mason updates. Sign up here: *davidarcherbooks.com/alex-updates*

ALSO BY DAVID ARCHER & BLAKE BANNER

To see what else we have to offer, please visit our respective websites.

www.davidarcherbooks.com
www.blakerbanner.com

Thank you once again for reading our work!

---

[1]

See *Brotherhood of the Goat*

Made in the USA
Columbia, SC
26 January 2024